THE 8TH
RANK

BIG BAD MAGIC SERIES

ROSE SINCLAIR

ISBN: 978-1-7359375-1-9
Art Over Chaos Publishing
artoverchaos.com

To my past self, thank you for getting me here.

BIG BAD WONDERLAND

QUEEN OF HEARTS'
SPRING CASTLE

SHERWOOD FOREST

SNOW WHITE &
CHARMING'S CASTLE

FROG PRINCE'S
CASTLE

THE
BRIAR
COAST

QUEEN OF HEARTS'
WINTER CASTLE

PRINCE PHILIP'S
CASTLE

RAPUNZEL'S
TOWER

THE CANDY
COTTAGE

N

BEAST'S TOWN

THE BEANSTALK
GROVE

Part One: Upon The Shore
Prologue

Four simple words have defined my life: Once upon a time. Where Queens become pawns, and the most dangerous pieces on the board can be captured.

Patches of dead grass trailed behind my boots. The death that echoed my steps was the start of the curse. I walked toward the only other figure on this desolate field. The gold-trimmed uniform of the royal guard clung to her closer than an animal's pelt. Her red cloak blowing behind her softly in the wind as the bottom edge kissed the grass below.

"What was it you said before?" She taunted. Her voice carrying over the distance forcefully. "The better to end you with?"

"Old fables won't help you." My hand jerked out sharply, preparing a spell. I felt the energy gather around my fingers before cascading ribbons of magic crackled like lightning. Erupting in smoke in my palm.

She raised her arm over her face to block the twisting

shadows. Energy surely growing strong in her own veins fueled by a desire to control. Magic ate a path on the grass as it raced forward. Gold sparks splintered violently off an invisible shield in front of her. "You could have been my Lieutenant, Malcolm." Her voice echoed in my head as the building magic tides distorted sound and reality around us. "We could have ruled. Yet you still refuse my olive branch."

Further taunts from someone more a politician than a mage in her own right. I had no words left as anger rose in my throat. It spilled out of my mouth in a yell.

The ground quaked. The sun seemed to flicker away for a few drawn out seconds, dimming everything around us but the smokey magic pouring out from my form.

She took a step back, forced into the motion. The conflicting currents consumed the remaining grass, and the ends of her riding cape. Magic consumed, and it came for every bone and muscle in me.

Her shield cracked, falling around her in torn streamers. Their glittering bits turned to ash as my spell powered past, starting at her fingertips then rolling over her arm, turning everything it could touch into stone. Her eyes flashed bright yellow before dimming to that same gray.

Chapter One

My thoughts cut in and out as my eyes burned and waves pushed me about. My fingers dug into wet sand. The sensation providing enough lucidity for me to gain control of my body again.

Rooftops and chimneys blurred in the distance. A flash of houses before my world wobbled with a wave of dizziness. I looked over my shoulder, back toward the ocean that spit me out. A few shells and large rocks dotted the landscape on the beach. A wave crashed against me, and I worked on standing.

I blinked up at the town which was alive with steady puffs from scattered chimneys. The buildings nearest the shore were a single story, with a few larger ones dotting the skyline behind them. "Where am I?" I muttered.

Half-convinced I was in a dream, I wandered up to a cobblestone path then down a small line of shops. The new details weren't adding up to anything. I had been... in a field.

A headache broke the thought and all I could do was

ride the wave of pain out. Something else touched me then. With a twitch, I forced my eyes open again to lash out at whatever it was, only to find a colorful ball sitting there.

"Sorry about that." I turned to see a man standing with a child, who couldn't be older than ten. Her attention was on her wayward toy, while his remained on me. "Sophie got a bit overzealous there."

"It's okay." For a second, I thought I might stare at the muscular man until Sophie moved to grab her ball from around my feet. They must be related given the similar softness of their faces. He was a little young to be married with a wife and child. Siblings, maybe? "Actually, could you tell me where this is?"

"The Briar Coast." He answered, eyes narrowing when I clearly must have looked as clueless as before. "Past the wall and as far west you can go without a boat. You aren't just a lost traveler, are you?"

Everything in my gut yelled run. But with a quick glance around I didn't know where I could. It all looked like coastline and more town. "I think I was in a fight."

"A shipwreck is more likely," Sophie declared. She trained her eyes on my soaked clothes.

He gave Sophie a warning look before softly giving me a smile. "Maybe if we start over it will help. My name is Jonathan. We live around here. What is your name?"

I opened my mouth. And to my horror no sound came, only the headache threatening to come back stronger. "Malcolm. That's my name."

"That's a good start. If you were part of a wreck, I'm sure we'll hear details of it soon. Maybe that will help you put more together. Let us show you where the inn is so you have somewhere to stay."

"Can Mal join us for lunch?" Sophie asked.

It was if she was the world's tiniest wing man making sure our paths didn't part before this dream at least got interesting.

If Jonathan was debating letting a stranger join them for lunch, I didn't catch it. A 'no' would have been dreadfully awkward so maybe he just wanted to save himself the embarrassment. "Seems only fair since Sophie did kick a ball at you."

"I didn't mean to," Sophie mumbled.

The fact that she was even still here and not spirited away after serving a purpose started to convince me this wasn't a dream. Which just added to my overall confusion.

I must have looked out of it because when Jonathan spoke again, he seemed worried. "If you want that is. We can try to take you to a doctor or something else if you need."

"No, lunch would be great thank you." If I was stranded somewhere, I rather it be with people who offered meals to poor washed-up souls.

Only seconds after agreeing Sophie grabbed my hand and gave me a little tug in the direction she wanted. As we walked towards their house, she pointed out all the places in her life that she deemed important. I didn't know if she thought they might trigger my own memories or if she just wanted me to know.

The strangest detail, and the only thing even vaguely dream or afterlife-like was a path that led to an old house owned by a man who believed in magic. Jonathan rolled his eyes at this part of the story. My thoughts were slowed by the realization that they didn't think magic was real.

Every time I tried to reach for the details from before today it felt untouchable. Like even if I could reach it my hand would grasp onto nothing.

"And this is our house," Sophie declared, finally letting go of my hand as we walked up to the door. I had to take an extra-long step over shoes littered at the entrance. From their size, Sophie's. A dirty dish from the table was moved in a nervous haste by Jonathan.

Was he being bashful? Or did he just think I'd judge his place for not being perfect? I sure wished it were the first, despite not feeling much of a catch right now being equally clueless as soaked.

"Go wash up for lunch," Jonathan prompted Sophie. She pouted for a second, but when it didn't work, she gave up and headed off to I assume the bathroom.

"I'm sorry if this is overwhelming. She's a handful." Jonathan said with a nervous laugh before walking into the kitchen.

"She's cute." I followed him because I didn't know where to be or go. "Is she your…"

"Sister." He quickly added as his weight shifted uncomfortably.

Before I had time to even guess why or ask a follow up Sophie presented herself back in the room. "What are you guys talking about?"

"Nothing." Jonathan gestured for her to take a seat.

I worried that lunch would be uncomfortable, but Sophie was a chatterbox that changed subjects quickly, making sure no one could be bored or discuss anything to the point of discourse.

That is until I chimed in after she mentioned magic again. "Maybe that old man can help me remember something."

"That guy?" Jonathan asked dismissively. Maybe even more than he meant since he seemed to backpedal. "He's just so… eccentric."

I worked on burying my daydreams of playing house under my vegetables. Magic is real. I must have done it.

"Geez, I'm outnumbered now," Jonathan said playfully but it was a tone that worked to cheer Sophie up more than me. "The magic believers outnumber me now."

After lunch Sophie wiggled her away out of doing the dishes, leaving Jonathan and I alone again. "Look, I'm sorry." He held his hand out for my plate. "I didn't mean to shoot your idea down."

"It's fine."

"No, it's not." He brought the plates to the sink before stealing the seat next to me that Sophie had been in before. "If I invite you to stay with us, will you promise not to think I'm some closed-minded town folk?"

"I wasn't thinking that." Maybe he did know something I didn't. From further away his eyes looked blue like the ocean, but up close they were this lively shade of green. I had been thinking and making assumptions about who he was and started to feel a little guilty about it. Figuring out who I was had to be number one. And maybe even the second and third thing too. "But it's a deal."

Jonathan smiled a little before he stood. "I would consider it a personal favor if you curbed the magic talk for a while. I don't want Sophie to think that magic is the solution to all her problems."

That I understood. Whatever happened to me I was sure it was because of magic. More might make my memory problems worse.

I did nothing for a while. A few days maybe, but I didn't want to think about how much time passed. Every day would go about the same, made up of wandering down towards the docks where Jonathan worked. He had assured me being this close to water if there were any shipwrecks in the area everyone at the docks would be the first to hear about it. Realistically, a theory I didn't believe anymore.

Jonathan was in view loading crates onto a carriage. He must have spotted me because once finished he headed over. "Hey Mal." He wiped his hands clean against his pants. "Keeping yourself entertained?"

"Not in the slightest."

He laughed. "Well, I heard something interesting," he teased before heading over to a docked ship to grab another crate.

"Hey! Wait," I followed him, and was tricked into manual labor to hear the rest of the story. I didn't care what was in this box, if the news was about another mermaid sighting, I was dropping it and never asking sailors for tips ever again.

"The Queen is missing."

"The Red Queen?"

Jonathan heaved his box onto a stack of others. "Is that what you call The Queen of Hearts where you are from?" It was nice he considered I was right, in my own way, rather than outright correcting me, before taking the crate I was carrying and adding it to the growing pile. Both of which were nice, but also felt wrong.

Once the news hit the town it spread quickly. Whispers came into focus with my growing context. Some people were happy. The Queen of Hearts sought the heads of both her sworn enemies and anyone who accidentally crossed her. Blind fury did not gain one extra friends. Sovereign or not. People were afraid. With no queen, people feared the Riders. Said no one would be able to keep them in check now.

"Do they know who did it?"

Jonathan shrugged. "Maybe one of the princesses wanted a fancier crown. It doesn't matter. There's a reward. They are giving money to people to travel to find news of her whereabouts."

"Oh, come on. If you aren't prepared for a journey like that, you'll drown in it all. A queen just doesn't get lost. And I doubt will simply be found. I met her once, that isn't her style."

Only after Jonathan froze, did I realize the importance of what I said. He spoke slowly as if any fast movements would scare off the memory. "You met her?"

I ignored his question for a moment. It was as clear as breakfast this morning. The throne room, a wide and flowing red dress. Guards lining the walls like a deck of cards flushed out. Another hooded woman in red. Standing right of the Queen. I hadn't been fighting the Queen of Hearts. Who was the other person?

"Mal. What do you remember?"

When I looked at Jonathan again the image drifted away, as if carried past me. "I— I'm sorry I lost it."

"Don't worry. It is still proof things are coming back to you. All you needed was a bit of *real* magic. Time."

Chapter Two

Time is not divine, it erodes.

I wasn't sure what was real anymore. Being here made that battle on the hill feel like a distant nightmare. But if magic wasn't real, why not try to live happily on the coast?

It didn't help that despite still not believing in magic, Jonathan wanted to find the Queen. Making any attempts at picturing a quiet life here unstable. I didn't understand his motivation. Maybe he felt haunted with all the memories he had here and had just been waiting silently for an out.

We had one clue, no matter how far-fetched it was. *Me.*

One early morning, I headed into Jonathan's room having made a choice for myself. I stopped in the doorway, startled as I caught him pulling on his shirt. Working in the shipyards six days a week paid off. He was an impressive sight shirtless.

"Oh, hey Mal," he said, casually lifting his gaze to me.

After kicking my head into proper focus, I blurted what I came here to say. "I'm going to see that strange old man."

"Alright." I couldn't read his tone, but a yes was a yes. "I actually want to go with you. And we'll have to take Sophie, or I'll never hear the end of it."

He gathered some fruit to eat, and as Sophie heard of the plan, she nearly pushed us out the door. Along the way I was tossed an apple as my share. I avoided dropping it by catching it out of pure reflex. The pristine red skin glistened up at me and my throat tightened as if to tell me not to eat it. But I couldn't place why, so feigned that I wasn't hungry until we were there.

The odd house didn't match the others in town. This one had a huge solid wooden door borrowed from a tree that would have to be timelessly old to be thick enough. Colored glass beads were placed in the knots of the wood for privacy.

Light was blocked from the green one, then the blue one, as if someone were looking through them. I raised my hand to knock but the door swung open before I touched it.

A man with a long white beard that reached the middle of his chest stood before us. "You can't show up at my door like a bunch of animals," he scolded.

The comment, just like the apple, felt wrong. An annoyance that was building in my chest like a young fire.

A recognition in the old man's eyes ended with a finger pointed at me. "You're the one who washed up on the beach."

"The man in question."

"Ah, so not a mermaid," he said, sounding even more curious with that outcome than if I had been.

"Mermaids?" Sophie asked.

"They don't share the same genders as us." He looked off for a moment. "Of course, I haven't met every mermaid, so shouldn't declare such things."

Jonathan just watched for a second before clearing his throat. "I don't know if you remember me."

The old man ushered us in, closing the door before his attention fell fully on Jonathan and Sophie. "I know everyone who lives in town. You all can call me Myrddin," he said then turned to me. "And you?"

"Came for a reason."

Myrddin glanced away, back to the siblings. "This one has a bite, aye?" When they didn't seem to agree he gave me his attention again. "Ask your questions then."

"I need help deciphering a memory."

"It may help us find the Queen of Hearts,"

Now Myrddin shared a knowing look with me. But what I was meant to know was beyond me. "Do you believe in magic?"

I didn't want to be the first to answer, but Jonathan seemed to be avoiding the question, and Sophie too distracted by his cluttered house of thingmabobs. "I don't know what to believe."

"And the rest of you?"

I could feel Jonathan's weary look, almost hear his suspicion even without a word. "I do!" Sophie raised her hand into the air like she was in class.

"This calls for a test," Myrddin declared and wandered off to the other end of the room. With some digging, he turned back to us with a doll in his hands. "Here we go." He held a palm open and flat, and when he moved his other hand away the doll floated.

More than that. It started to twirl. He quickly closed his hand, ending it all. "Now you."

"Me?" I struggled to spit out another word as he pressed the doll to my hand. "I don't want this. Aren't you meant to explain the trick beforehand?"

"If it had been a trick."

I tried to set the toy on her feet, but without my other hand propping it up even that was a fight. An owl cooed loudly outside drawing Sophie's attention. Both of ours really. Only Jonathan was focusing on what we've been shown. Me and the doll. My grip tightened into a fist, crushing the dress as I grew more annoyed. "I don't play with dolls."

"You need to believe in it. Back when you believed anything in the world was possible."

"Fine," I growled. Closing my eyes and focusing everything in me on the weight in my hand. Imagining what it would look like floating here instead of with the old mage. Then I pictured being able to see the air swirling around the doll.

"Wonderful!" Myrddin exclaimed. The distraction caused the doll to fall back into my hand before I even opened my eyes to see it work. "Few can make it go on the first try. Magic must have already carved its way through you."

I doubted I had actually done anything. But the ends of the doll's dress was singed up close. Had it always been like that? I tossed the toy down on the nearest surface. "This isn't what we are here for. Can you help me decipher a memory?"

"Red enhances details." Myrddin's eyes were elsewhere. A gray color that matched the sea on a stormy day and seemed just as likely to change. "Blue effects creativity."

Lost, I looked to Jonathan. Who just shook his head and shrugged as Myrddin went on to say that not all reds were the same.

The old man at least agreed with himself and moved over to a bookshelf. His index finger moved about the spines, following a pattern that was only apparent to him. Some of the books had a thin band of color in lieu of title.

He plucked one and sprawled it on a table. Inside was swatches of every shade of red one could imagine, if not more. "Find the one you saw."

"How do you know—"

"Focus." He tapped the book.

I flipped through pages and pages of red that hardly seemed different. After a bit Sophie reached over and took the doll to play with. I tried to ignore her, but soon her humming distracted me further as she gave up on the magical route and just played the old fashion way.

Not happy with hibiscus, mahogany, red wine, or burgundy. The pages blended into each other until a scarlet color stood out. It made me see a yellow shade. The reflected color in her eyes. But the goldish glow wasn't her color. It was mine. With a gasp the memory filled my mind. The taunts, the sensation of being someone powerful.

When I exhaled, a new memory took its place. "Take these unsavory men away from me!" the Queen of Hearts demanded, dismissing us with a wave of her hand.

Red walked down the steps grabbing my arm to pull me up to my feet. "What a big mouth full of lies you have." Her words painted me the same color that was only her behavior.

I pulled away quickly, not allowing her to touch further. Glaring, and unable to hold my tongue. "The better to end this now."

Myrddin leaned in over my shoulder. Breaking the

16

flashback as reality crashed back into center focus. "That shade belongs to a group known as the Riders. It's the color of their capes."

"Where do they fit into things?" Jonathan asked.

Myrddin moved away to grab a pencil and the nearest piece of paper. On it he drew a circle. "This is the Riders." He drew another circle that intercepted the first. "This is your Queen and her Cards." Then finished a much smaller circle placed near the bottom but didn't touch any other.

"Where are the rest of the royals?" Jonathan asked, while I tried to place the unnamed circle.

Myrddin nodded at the question. With a dash, he made a straight line through the bottom of the bigger two circles. "The Nine." I couldn't tell if the line was meant to touch the last circle, or if he had simply drawn his example too small.

"Why did I have a meeting with the Queen of Hearts?"

Myrddin looked amused as he nearly closed the book on my hand and placed it back on the shelf. "Could be an endless number of possibilities," he said, "From my perch here, I have no way of seeing such things."

My manners must have washed up on a different shore without me because his selective magical lucidity was growing tiresome. I wanted to shake more answers out of him, but doubted I'd be given another night in Jonathan's spare bed if I threatened people. Even someone he wasn't that fond of.

I closed my eyes in an attempt to calm myself. All I could think about was how magic wasn't only real. It was abundant. "Was I a Rider?"

Myrddin came back over from his bookshelf. His age gave him quite the height advantage. A difference made even more severe given that I was sitting. He placed cool hands on each side of my face, turning my head a bit before grabbing my jaw. With a finger he lifted my upper lip as if privy to dental records. His hand fell away. "I've seen Riders before. You aren't one I remember."

"Oh." Somehow that didn't seem to disappoint me.

Instead of adding anything, Myrddin already had moved on. Attention now on Sophie as she played. "I think you should keep that doll. She needs a friend."

"Really? Thank you!" She squeezed in a quick hug before she looked down at the gift. "Is she the magic, or are only people magic?"

"Ah, now that is the question you have to figure out."

Jonathan's own tolerance seemed to be failing as he let out a frustrated sigh. Likely after not getting a say in if Sophie got to bring possibly magical objects into the house or not. "Toys, but no information that will help us find the Queen of Hearts."

"Now that's positively not true." For the first time Myrddin sounded offended. "Is it, Malcolm?"

I didn't want to come to his aid after he manhandled me in such an unceremonious way. But he was right. If I wasn't a Rider but had an audience with the Queen: Either I could be a failed one who fought with leadership, or part of that unnamed group that was tangled up with royalty all the same.

Chapter Three

"I did not realize you knew how to cook," Jonathan said as he caught me making a meal.

"Does it count as knowing how to cook if it's just following directions?" I thought having next to no memories would make cooking hard. What if something was secretly poison if eaten raw? But turns out recipes were just as easy as magic.

"I'd say so. Took me years to do anything more than burn water."

Despite being next to sure that was impossible, Jonathan looked serious enough that I wondered if he could burn water as easy as toast. Who knew, I could do things I didn't even dare to mention to him.

Sophie came down the stairs with leaps and bounds. "Are we going to meet a princess? Or the Queen!" Sophie asked, backpack in her hand dragging behind her.

"What's going on?"

"Well, Sophie loves an adventure," Jonathan said, trying

to sell this to me like I assumed he once tried to use on his parents. I cared less about pleasing a tiny child than anyone else here, so he quickly changed his tactic. "I want to help find the Queen. I want the reward. To travel. See more than the sea. With you, I think we can do it."

"Yeah!" Sophie added.

Meanwhile, I was nursing the small pang in my chest. 'With you', meaning some new memory might roll out of my head that would be helpful. Not 'with you', as a person because you're cute and I want to smush my face against yours. Did I really want to travel around with a hopelessly straight guy and his kid sister to find some stuffy lost Queen who didn't even like me?

Sophie stomped her foot once. "You have to come with us! Please don't make me eat nothing but found nuts and berries the whole time."

"Hey," Jonathan objected. "I know how to cook some things over a campfire." He smiled over to me. "Are you really going to fight us about this? Rather stay here, alone?"

That was definitely worse. I laughed despite myself. "Forget this small town, you want to find royalty? Pick a castle, and boom. Easy."

"Yeah!!" Sophie cheered. "I'd love to be a queen someday, wouldn't you?"

I guess the gendering could work depending on who you talked to. Puffy dresses and dripping jewelry filled my imagination. Maybe not. But the appeal of wanting to grow up into something shining and fabulous? I could buy into that.

We headed down to the docks which were full of people running from boats to carriages arms full. It felt like a chaotic pattern, but not to Jonathan as he read their movements like a line of text. "Follow me," he declared and was off.

I broke into a sprint to catch up to a carriage. Worry that Sophie would fall behind was misplaced since she proved to be quicker than me.

"Can we steal a ride from you?" Jonathan called up to the driver.

A straw-haired man looked us over as we fell into place along an invisible line. "What are friends for? Hop on the back."

"Up you go, cutie pie." Jonathan picked up Sophie and sat her on the back. She leaned against a wooden crate with her feet happily kicking off the end. He offered his hand to me next with a formality that verged on playful.

"Thanks." With one foot on the bar below, I popped up near Sophie. Jonathan hopped up next, with a stolen glance to see if the driver needed anything.

The carriage pulled forward with an unexpected start. I didn't mind the bumps or the sound of hoofs that allowed for our travel given the speed it gained us.

We stopped before nightfall at a store that served as a connecting point for three towns. Least that's all I was told before Jonathan gestured us to head inside while he lent our driver a hand.

I walked around with Sophie, checking to see what we might need to pick up before going any farther. We had the basics but anything else was tricky to plan for. Soon we both became distracted by the less serious offerings. We also couldn't afford anything too fancy, and only ended up with some dried fruit.

"Alright, I'm back." Jonathan was out of breath as he caught up to us. "We need a ride change to go further. There's another trader heading to the wall and said we could tag along since it's a light shipment."

I nodded as we paid for our things as if I knew where he meant. Forward at least, and forward was good.

I climbed in and stopped short at all of the space we were given. While our first ride was clearly a favor, this one likely didn't trouble the driver or horse at all. A total of five small crates were tucked together. Sophie sat against the back and quickly failed staying awake.

"Where are we going again?"

Jonathan settled, having to watch his head the whole time. "I've only heard about it in tales, but apparently there is this giant wall of rose bushes. I've been told they are so tall they reach the clouds."

I smiled. "That part must be a myth."

"I must confess," he said, stealing a look over at his now dreaming sister. "I'm eager to find out."

We stopped at a gate the next morning and watched the driver go further without us. In front of us on both sides was those impressively tall rose bushes. They didn't reach the sky, but it definitely looked as if the thorns would rip you to several pieces before you climbed over.

Something shined on top of the wall ahead of us, and curiosity caused my feet to speed up. Once close, I realized a man was sitting there, unharmed with a pale white bald head and a bow tie.

"Don't the thorns hurt?" I asked, craning my neck to see him.

"I have a thick shell that doesn't crack easily." The man leaned forward slightly, his hands pressing into the bush. "My name's Humphrey Duncan. What might your names be?"

We introduced ourselves, and he nodded in consideration. "What do your names mean?"

"Must they mean anything?" I asked.

"With names like that you might be almost anyone. Every word has meaning."

Sophie glanced over to us, then looked all the way up at the strange man. "Why are you sitting alone, Humphrey?"

"Because there is no one here with me." Humphrey broke into a smile. "How old did you say you were?"

Sophie grinned. "Ten!"

"Wrong," he said to her confusion. "You didn't say."

Jonathan sighed. "She thought you meant how old."

"Why do you keep playing with our words like that?" I raised a hand to help block the sun from my eyes. "You knew what she meant."

"It's my job," he said proudly and set his chin in a high pose. "Words mean what people choose them too. You should keep that lesson in mind lest you become declawed like another animal I might mention."

My chest tightened. "What animal?"

He looked down at us again. "The Big Bad Wolf, of course. First him, and then the Queen. I'm glad she paid me early."

Jonathan took a step to leave but didn't make it far

before his curiosity caught him. "What exactly did you do for them?"

"I wrote the law. The nine ruling families signed a treaty. Some did it for love, some fear. Others, both. But signed they did. It promised to grant freedom but was interpreted to make them all Cards of the Queen."

"Could you tell us where to find the Queen now?" Jonathan asked.

Humphrey's bald head caught the light again as he leaned back. "A person can find anything within their heart."

I was debating just hurling something at him, so he'd fall off. That would surely put an end to his wordplay and get us a clearer answer. But remembered I was traveling with a child. "Aren't you boiling up there? What are you waiting for?"

"Work."

"Is this the right direction?"

"Yes."

"Wonderful." I gripped the straps of my bag tightly and started walking.

"That it is." He chuckled to himself. "Anywhere you go in this wonderland is wonderful."

Jonathan silently started following me, and I heard Sophie a step behind us. "I guess we are going, bye!"

"Don't mind him," Sophie said. She took Jonathan's hand, then glanced over to me, offering the other. "He was eggtremely weird."

I shook my head, wanting to hate what she said, but I did love puns. Damn it.

Chapter Four

"Shouldn't we be looking for the Queen? Instead of well, this?" We must have walked for miles until the new voice carried over to us from a gap in the briar's wall.

"We follow the local prince now until her return," another said.

Two men were posted with water cans at bushes that were newer than the rest. Over the knee-high barrier, I saw a black heart stitched onto their uniforms. The Queen's Cards.

"But these are white roses, that wasn't what—" The Card silenced himself when he noticed us. "Great, and now there are witnesses to your mistake."

The other guard looked nervously at us before turning back to his partner in horror. "My mistake?"

Jonathan held his hands up. "We saw nothing. Just walking by."

"I actually like the white ones," Sophie added. "They are nice after so many red roses this whole time."

The men whispered to each other.

"If you can't replant them," I tried to offer. "Can't you just use a bit of magic to change the color?"

The Cards turned to stare at me. "Do you know nothing about magic in this kingdom?"

I turned away to them to mouth 'Run' to Jonathan. He didn't follow exactly as suggested, but instead gave Sophie a little push away.

"But—" Sophie started to say before her brother cut her off with another push.

A Card climbed over the bushes to follow, but I stepped in the path to block him further. "Why don't you just replant them?"

"By royal decree—"

I ignored him, glancing over my shoulder happy to see Jonathan and Sophie were now booking it. "Right, where were we?"

"All witnesses must be taken to the prince." The other Card behind the shrubbery said. He tried to climb over, but quickly fell back. "Shit, ow!" As he pulled his hand back red blood dripped on a few white petals.

"What was that about witnesses?" I smirked, sizing the Cards up. If I took on Red, surely even now I could take two hapless peons. Though perhaps that wouldn't be prudent.

This was either the best idea, or the worst idea I ever had. Instead of fighting, I figured just letting the men take me to the prince would be best. We three were the only ones who knew about Jonathan and Sophie so if the Cards stayed busy for longer all the better.

Plus, it made me feel better about not having quickly figured out how to draw on magic in the first place. I doubted doll spinning skills translated well to combat.

On horseback, the castle quickly came into view. Made up of several small blue peaks that were just a stone or two taller than the last. As if trying to just barely surpass the previous record.

We stopped at the stables where a handful of Cards were flush against the side waiting for orders. Other staff seemed to be more concerned about them then having a stranger ride in.

A man stepped out. His brown tunic matched his hair as if they had been specifically picked out to do so. His black undershirt brought out the bags under his eyes. "What's going on here?" The accent suggested aristocracy.

"There was a mistake with the wall. We brought the witness to you, Prince Phillip." The Card I was sharing a horse with said, before dismounting.

"Actually, there were three witnesses," the second said. A clear attempt to throw the other into deep trouble.

"What's wrong with the wall?"

"The roses are white, sir." The Card's head hung low. "Please don't use our blood to paint them."

Someone in the group of servants behind him gasped. The Prince turned to her briefly then back with a frown on his face. "None of that is going to happen. Please excuse yourself from my sight."

The Cards hurried over to the others waiting as if shuffling in would keep them safe.

After a brief thought of stealing the horse and running off curiosity got the best of me. I got off and stood in front of the Prince. "Is there a reason your men fear you so?"

"My men?" he repeated, then sighed. "Follow me, I have much to explain. You had others with you?"

"No."

Prince Phillip turned to me. Taking a moment to study me from head to toe. I don't know what he decided but without another word he turned and walked inside his castle.

Just like the recipes earlier that day, I did as told. I wished for another moment to take in the heroic scenes painted about, or the tall ceilings trimmed with sparkling chandeliers. A single spoon in this place might be worth more than a week's wages at the shipyards. And Phillip only one of the many princes. Maybe Jonathan had been too vague about the reward.

The Prince walked with easy steps bringing us past his throne which was made out of red oak carved into flowers that wrapped around the chair's feet. It was striking even without its owner seated.

He brought us to a side room with a large table that could hold several people. A desk with papers loomed in the back. A single man stood guard, completely still as if a statue.

Phillip took the chair at the head of the table, motioning for me to take the one to his left. I did, fearing where this conversation was going. "What misconceptions about my land do I need to repair?"

If he had a glowing reputation it wasn't known by me in the first place. I glanced over to where the guard was stationed. This man didn't have a heart, spade, or any suit on his chest. "If Cards belong to the Queen, why are they outside?"

"Since her disappearance, they have nowhere to return. They act rash, but so many hearts otherwise suit me." He smiled at his joke.

"The Cards believed you'd kill them because they planted white roses when you requested red."

"Do you see me as a monster?"

If he was offended, his look was too practiced to spot anything besides a careful neutral. "I wasn't trying to suggest that."

"Either you don't know, or don't believe the tales." He pushed out of his chair, the legs dragging on the ground without formality. "I shall show you the truth."

He brought me to the east wing of the castle in silence. My eyes trailed down the long hall that could have been the whole wing, and I spotted a sleeping woman on a bed as detailed as the throne. "Aurora," Phillip breathed. "My princess."

Can't a guy find a single prince around here? My dismay was quickly replaced with noticing something curious. Her chest was completely still. Her hair was gold like spun silk, her face pleasant as if blissfully dreaming of the prince that waited for her. Arms folded over her chest with a single red rose in her grasp.

"The lands are barren because all the magic from them is gone. Any found is funneled here." As the Prince went on his voice seemed more and more distant. "She was poisoned, and we couldn't find a cure. Magical or otherwise. All I could do was stop time to halt the poison but messing with time is very costly."

That's why all of the Cards in this area were hearts. They tasked themselves to help mend a broken one. But Prince Philip had a much softer hand than a ruthless queen.

"Sir?" A voice echoed down towards us, as a guard kept a respectful distance. "More… guests are here."

"Your friends, I'm assuming?"

I held my tongue. Not giving away anything until I spotted Jonathan and Sophie waiting by a woman with an apron no worse for wear.

Sophie ran over when she spotted me. "We were worried about you! So, I thought pick a castle, boom, royal."

"I'm glad to see you are both okay." I looked over to Jonathan trying to silently ask him how and why he was here.

"A bit down the way we found some of the Prince's men. They apologized at great length and said we should come to find you."

"About that," Prince Phillip said sternly. "I need to have another discussion with the Cards. If you will excuse me."

The woman in the apron bowed as the Prince left, then held out a hand to Sophie. "Come on let's get you cleaned up, and then we can play dress up in the Princess's closet."

"This seems as good as a spot to stay for the night as any," Jonathan said. He kept Sophie in view as he spoke to me. "I don't know how many buildings we will get to sleep in. Let alone, castles. That okay with you?"

I nodded. "Let Sophie have fun while she can."

"Thanks," Jonathan added, before trailing after them.

Sleep was impossible for me that night. I think the Cards made everyone feel like a prisoner. Even if it was their own home. The design of the castle caused me to wander down the same long hallway that led to the Princess. This time another figure was silhouetted in candlelight.

I don't think I was meant to come in here, but it felt as destined as making that doll spin. Instead of leaving I took careful steps towards the figure and the Prince's tired eyes lifted to me. "Couldn't sleep either?"

The Prince shook his head slightly. "Jonathan told me about you. That you can't remember who you were. I'd help if I could, but it seems all I can do is keep things the same."

Orange-red light from the candles in the room danced almost above Aurora's face as if nothing in the world could touch her. "Is that why you signed the Treaty of the Nine?"

"You know a lot for someone who claims to know nothing."

I laughed to myself. "I don't mean to alarm you but there's a man sitting on your giant rose wall."

He inhaled deeply, eyes lifting to the ceiling for a moment. "Yet another unfortunate event caused by the Queen's disappearance. He wrote the treaty. I think he believes if he doesn't fall, being up there keeps him safe from any of its effects.

"You are right, however. If I hadn't agreed, the Queen would have tightened her grip. I honestly only care about one thing anymore."

His voice trailed off. I'm not even sure if he knew he said the last of those words aloud. Shadows from the candlelight caressed his angular face. How I wished I had woken up under the wistful longing of someone who loved me. Maybe my own yearning was what caused me to speak without thinking about the words leaving my mouth. "You should let her go."

Prince Phillip met my eyes. I saw something reflected

there. Not colorful magic like before, but something darker. "And you should do something about the treaty."

"Me? I'm no one."

"Exactly. You are free from attachments that cause bias. Won't have your mind clouded by what was, that's what stops people from seeing what could be."

The next morning, I found out that the Prince had ordered his seamstresses to make everyone more suitable traveling clothes. Deeming ours good enough for the coast, but unsuitable for any other terrain further east.

In a whirlwind, I had to pick fabric, color, and a dozen other things I didn't quite follow as maids danced around me taking measurements. They worked dizzyingly fast, but without magic still took most of the afternoon to outfit the trio of us.

Sophie had been sitting outside my room swinging her feet idly as she waited. "Come on let's go find that brother of yours," I said, offering my hand.

"He's in the throne room."

"You are a helpful kid; don't let anyone tell you different."

"I won't."

We found Prince Phillip and Jonathan huddled together. Speaking to each other over a small box in view of both of them.

"What do you have?" Sophie lifted to her tippy toes to see a music box in the Prince's hands. The sides were painted with colorful dancers and trimmed with gold feet and jewels. The lid was white with a crest proudly displayed in the center.

"I have little communication with those outside the wall," Prince Phillip said. "This is the only other magic that remains." He turned the box around and waited for me to step closer. From this side a figure wore pink, and her dance partner bore a resemblance to him. "This delivers news to whoever holds it. I believe this morning's message is relevant to your journey."

I carefully took it from his hands, and a soft lullaby started to play and a tiny mirror behind the couple fogged up. Shapes formed and I realized the smoke made words. "An eye for an eye. A Queen for a Queen. The merry men move at dawn. Making the monarch their pawn. Instead of seeing a new day. They wish to make her pay." Were we actually fated to save the Queen?

"What do we do to help?" Jonathan said, ready to pounce on his new royal task.

Phillip started to shake his head, before taking a second. "The Frog Prince has more powerful mirrors. He might be able to see these merry men and tell you exactly where they are."

"Then that's where we shall go."

"A group that takes a Queen against her will shouldn't be fully trusted."

"For Queen and country then," Jonathan mused.

"I've prepared horses for you," Phillip said. "They are at the stables waiting, you'll find a map of the surrounding lands in the saddle."

"Who are these merry men?" I asked.

"I've only heard rumors of a group of bandits that live

in the forests. Stealing when they venture out."

"Thank you for everything," Jonathan said.

"And you little one," Phillip said to Sophie. "Stay out of trouble for these two, all right?"

"I'll be on my best behavior," she promised.

Jonathan smiled and with a formal goodbye, we headed to the stables. Two horses had been set aside for us, and I started checking the saddlebag for the map. Not expecting, but still disappointed when I didn't see a marker that read "Malcolm's house and childhood memories here."

Sophie stared up at the horse, trying to figure out some wild idea on how to get on it without help. Equally as fruitless as my wishes. "I'm going to lift you up on three. Ready? One, two, up you go." Once settled I mounted my own horse. "If you get scared just give your brother a squeeze."

Riding was a joy compared to hitchhiking around the kingdoms. We road all day, then made camp under a canopy of trees that gave shade to a large patch of grass that would please both us and the horses for the night. I used the jacket the Prince demanded be made as a pillow and stared up at the stars that shined through the leaves wondering if they knew the future, or if we just made wishes.

Chapter Five

Smoke filled my nose. I opened my eyes to a dense forest as I coughed. Flashes of red could be seen darting in between the trees as people on horseback rode by. I knew two things watching them. They were the Queen's escort, and I was dreaming.

"Still don't trust her?" An amused voice said. He walked up to stand next to me. His rich brown hair and a fitted green tunic always managed to draw my attention.

Without a word from me, he drew an arrow out from his quiver. Lifting a bow that had wood burnt sigils engraved in it. Through the tree line, spotted the Queen, then the red riding hood of her second in command.

"Robin." The word tasted sweet in my mouth. Equally amused as it was a warning. "What will I ever do if you decide to let go?"

His teeth bit into his bottom lip, bow lowering, chance lost. Robin grinned to himself for a second turning to meet my gaze. "Why Mal, I'd never."

My stomach felt weak. What was a little regicide if it meant more time in the forest with him? A sense of duty and responsibility to keep others safe soured my big bad ideas. "Once we fix the treaty, I won't want to watch over them anymore."

"Sure." Robin nodded as he moved away, but the doubt was clear in his voice.

I scrambled to get up and follow him. Limbs not cooperating until I woke up for real with a jerking start. "Damn it, geez."

My mumbling caught Jonathan's eye. He was crouched over the dying fire from the night before that he was making sure was safe to leave behind. "You okay?"

"Just a bad dream."

He gave me a sympathetic look before going to wake Sophie, leaving me to feel guilty for lying. We'd have real answers soon. Not pieces I didn't know how to place in order.

The map we were given showed where the Frog Prince's castle was since his land was not marked off by any marker, shrubbery or otherwise.

His palace looked nothing like the towering keep of before. I only assumed we were close when I started to see Cards moving around. Just barely I could make out the black diamond stitched on their clothes. If the heart suit dealt with emotional needs, what was their purpose?

We rode on to an estate with damp stone walls covered in moss as if nature was its own tapestry.

"More suitors?" A Card at the door asked us. "The Frog Prince adores new visitors."

I glanced to Jonathan who looked equally clueless as to what to say. "Prince Phillip sent us." Strong answer.

Neutral. Doesn't commit to anything.

The Card ushered us into the keep where the room opened up with two pillars with large stone frogs sitting on top. A curly haired man sat on the throne with his feet lounging over the armrest. His sharp chin lifted. "Is she going to be my new princess?"

"What?" Jonathan said, and pushed Sophie behind him a bit more. "No. She's a child."

"Then you?" The Prince asked. "I've been waiting my whole life for the right person and here you all are." He smoothly got up from his throne and started to walk over to us. Love at first sight wasn't a magic I mastered, but I'd be willing to pretend if he wanted.

"Prince Phillip sent us for information about the Queen of Hearts' location." Jonathan thankfully explained as I wondered how soft his curls would be to the touch.

"My apologies." His hand lifted to wave off the last topic. "Normally when two men bring me a child, they want to sell her off. You buy one girl's freedom and suddenly everyone wants to cash in."

Sophie let out a small whine and hung onto Jonathan's shirt sleeve even tighter.

"Don't worry, little one," The Frog Prince said softly. "I prefer much – much older people."

I quickly tried to guess my own age. Before kicking myself and cleared my throat. "About the Queen of Hearts?"

Prince Henri had already turned and headed back to where he'd been seated before. "Gotten herself lost, has she? Can't say I care."

"Not even for the reward?" Jonathan asked.

A laugh bounced off the stone walls as if the room were

designed to make any of the Prince's word louder. "You can call me Henri. Who might you three be?"

"My name is Mal. This is Jonathan and Sophie." For Sophie's part she gave a tiny wave.

"Well Jonathan," Prince Henri said, carefully selecting his words this time. "If there was a reward, my Cards would have found her already. Diamonds are the suit of acquisition. I'm afraid you are on a quest for the morality of it."

"That's fine," Jonathan said, voice full of challenge.

I glanced at each of them for a moment, doubting anything would come from it. "Prince Phillip thought we could use your magic mirrors to find out where she was."

Henri sat forward, resting his chin on his hand, and clearly studying me for a moment. "Mal, was it? You're a curious one. Do you have a full name?"

"I just… know it's Malcolm."

His hum of acknowledgment was barely heard only for the room's layout. "If you aren't here as a suitor, and there's no reward. Why do you want to peer into the mirrors?"

"He has memories of the Queen." Sophie offered, and I tried not to wish she were too afraid to talk to him further.

I could have sworn his eyes shimmered in the light. "I do love a good story." Prince Henri gestured to a Card who stepped forward with a quick haste. "Ready the mirrors." With a bow the man went off as the Prince continued. "The smoke it takes to power them needs to build up in the room first. Come, we can wait around the waterfront."

He led us outside. Instead of a moat on three sides, there was a crystal-clear lake that had been unnaturally extended to wrap around the building. Complete with cattails and lily pads. Such details made me doubt this castle was for defense at all. Prince Henri might as well be a peacock showing off his colors to attract suitors. "Do you entertain often?"

Prince Henri tucked his hands neatly into his silk pockets. "It would be foolish of me to let the chance of love pass by."

"Surely there is no rush," Jonathan commented. I didn't know if he was still sore about the Sophie mix-up, or believed it.

The Prince didn't even seem to hear him as he went on. "They say love is the most powerful thing in the world," he said, eyes finding me. "And that we all must choose."

There it was. Another silent dare. I held his gaze for an extra moment, corner of my mouth smirking as I was sure I was reading him right. "I wouldn't if I didn't want to."

"Maybe that's why fate brought you here," Prince Henri said. He took my hand, lifting it to his lips. Soft and causing a shiver I worked on making unnoticeable.

Jonathan cleared his throat. I turned, expecting him to not like the show in front of Sophie. Instead, he was trying to bring our attention to the edge of the water where she was. A frog leaped away as we all looked. "How deep is that water?"

Prince Henri dropped my hand. Whistling loudly and was rewarded with Sophie's full attention. "Move away from the water unless you want to be part of your own fable."

This seemed to confuse Sophie more than anything, so she begrudgingly walked back up. "I was just trying to set my doll on the lily pad. She is more frog size."

I chuckled. "Why would you do that?"

Sophie looked at me funny. "The frog asked for a friend."

"A frog talked to you? Right, obviously."

42

Jonathan was less amused by everything. "How long until we can use your mirrors?"

"Should take until dinner time." He glanced towards me. "Unless you know of another way to power them faster."

"Only if a kiss holds a dose of magic like true love," I joked nervously.

The Frog Prince laughed again, softer, and more sincere than before.

When the sun set, we were brought to another wing of the estate into a large room without any windows. Full length mirrors stood near the back in an arch. Smoke filled the room up to the knee.

Compared to the last Prince's tiny mirror I expected something hand sized, not well, all of this. Only Henri was in the room with me. Jonathan and Sophie were told to wait outside. As well as any guard or aid. Prince Henri claimed that the more people in here would dilute the magic in the air faster.

I could taste it all on my tongue when I opened my mouth to speak. "What do all the mirrors do?"

"Some speak truth, some lie, and still others listen." Henri gestured me forward, towards a small platform somehow free of the smoke. A ring of salt circled the area and pillar candles were placed between the mirrors.

He carefully stepped over the salt ring and pointed down to the center. "Stand here."

I did so, soon becoming far too aware of all the reflections matching my every twitch. I saw the Prince, and myself, in each of their surfaces except one. We were both missing there.

No, that wasn't right. There was something sitting in the bottom of the mirror. An animal. I found my lips mouthing the answer: The Frog Prince.

"Wake." Commanded all of his reflections at once. My lungs seized in my chest, in a struggle to get air I gasped. Suffocating in so much smoke I could watch it as it poured into my mouth. Every mirror dimmed to a cold void and I thought my vision would follow.

"Show me love," Prince Henri said next. My consciousness flowed with his words as easy as the smoke did, and I became acutely aware that magic was being done to me. Rather than just watching it within the glass.

The mirror directly in front of us cleared. An image came into focus of someone in a green hood standing with a sword that was just under the throat of a woman. Her dress was white, layered with red that flowed over a throne. The large collar rose from the lace on her bodice reaching past her ears obscuring her form further. It didn't matter however, only the Queen of Hearts could afford such grandiose. "Do you wish to lose your head?" A practiced, mocking threat.

"Return our people," Robin demanded.

"I don't know where your little pet is." Her voice was different this time. Being held at the tip of a sword wasn't in her daily schedule. "Wasn't it enough to turn my right-hand to stone? You come and threaten my life too?"

Robin scoffed. "Take her." Shadows from the mirrors next to him moved. When they crossed to the one in the middle, they showed men hauling her away. The Queen's hands were tied, but otherwise untouched by magic.

"Show me this man's true name," Prince Henri said next,

taking images of Robin and his men away with a dizzying swirl. I reached for him and relaxed as a new memory came to me.

He was surrounded by a wintery forest. Animal pelt dotted with snow over his shoulders to keep him warm. He shrugged but was clearly amused with himself. "Come on. Who's afraid of a big bad wolf?"

I could see myself again. Not my reflection, but me, sitting there with a bow in my hands. The smell of wood burning filled my senses and when I was finished the bow was covered in fresh runes. "Please just take your weapon."

"Malcolm, I'm serious." Robin crouched down, one hand on the bow, but not quite taking it from me yet. "With a last name like Wolf you should have a fearsome reputation among those assholes who horde everything for themselves. People who are deemed as nice, never get to do anything else. But when you are intimidating no one fucks with you."

I leaned closer to him. Only a sliver of air existing between us. "Clearly not nobody, seeing as I'm helping you."

All my senses were within the image that when someone else spoke everything wobbled. "Mirror, where is this?"

"Sherwood Forest," I answered as smoke rolled out over my lips. My tongue darted out to taste it once more. I breathed in easy this time even as the images faded. So full of the intoxicating magic my eyes glowed. Two yellow points of light in the blackness.

Faintly aware as he moved off the platform. "End this."

I wasn't sure who he was talking to, but everything in the room still listened to him. The magic pulled out all the air within my lungs, and I collapsed, catching myself when I was on all fours. "Why did you do that?" I growled, feeling so disconnected from everything. As alone as I did when I woke up on the beach.

"You broke the salt line."

Not understanding, and half not wanting to I rolled my eyes and stood up. For the first time I felt more powerful than whatever his title granted him. "We are leaving."

"Not tonight you're not."

"Wait, explain it again," Jonathan said.

Sophie was sitting on one of the beds of our forced guest room trying to get her doll to spin around in her hand. "It's magic, it doesn't have to make sense."

I was at my wits end with both of them. Maybe even everyone. Getting my memories back felt so important, but now I was just angry. It wasn't the magic that didn't make sense it was the fragments of my life that only seemed to be getting a cutting edge to them.

"Let's just start over with the Queen. Is she okay?"

I picked at a seam of the chair I was in. "For now, it seems."

"And Prince Henri doesn't care?"

"All he said was that he signed her treaty. Said it wasn't his fault she was unable to wield the extra power she desired."

"Okay," Jonathan said, not appearing to believe me. "And we can't continue our journey tonight. Why?"

"For the last time, all he said was that the salt ring broke."

"Salt protects," Sophie offered. I turned suddenly looking at her as if she were babbling nonsense. "I mean, that's what I heard. I don't know."

I sighed, disappointed in myself and forced my feet to go over and say sorry. "Here, let me help."

Hesitatingly, she handed the toy over. It spun in my hand without more than half a thought. "Hold out your palm." She mirrored me and I tipped the doll into her hand. "Think of it like imagination in physical form. You have to believe you can do it, or nothing will happen."

The doll toppled as I moved my hand away. To her dismay, but Jonathan's audible sigh of relief. I ignored him and leaned in as if to tell her a secret. "What's something you wish for?"

Sophie pressed her lips together. Not wanting to ruin the wish, or maybe just not tell me. "Are you allowed to say?"

"Absolutely."

She moved to whisper in my ear. "I wish I could see something my parents did in their adventures. Before the storm…"

"As a way to be closer to them?"

Sophie looked down but nodded.

"It's a beautiful one, and beautiful things happen in this world. Remember that, okay?"

She nodded again, and I stood back up with a small smile to Jonathan's watchful eye. It was if he trusted and doubted me in equal measure as we went along our quest. The fact that I didn't know if I blamed him, made my skin itch. "I'm going to see if Prince Henri will reconsider."

"Alright."

After waiting a moment for anything else from him, I

left. Not even knowing where the Prince's rooms were. I considered asking a guard but decided I rather be alone. Everything grew darker and colder with nightfall.

Hours after I last saw the Prince, I found two Cards guarding a door that I figured must be where he was. Boredom more than anything caused me to ask for an audience with him. They turned to each other hopefully silently debating a yes. "I just want to talk."

"I'll go see if he wishes to see you," the one on the right replied before ducking into the room behind him.

I rocked back and forth on my heels trying to fill the wait with something. "What are diamonds tasked to do?" I asked, gesturing towards the four-pointed symbol on his chest.

Silence hung for a long moment.

"We are responsible for acquiring the desires of the Queen, or other royals."

"Ah, greed."

The guard's expression darkened.

"Your job suits you well." I laughed at my own joke, he didn't. Luckily, the first guard returned saving me from further awkwardness. "You can go in," he said, holding the door open.

I glanced at the other Card to make sure I hadn't offended him so much that he'd stop me as I walked in. He just stared forward again as if our conversation never happened in the first place.

The Prince's room was decorated entirely different than the others with green fabric hanging like a canopy. A large bed was placed against the wall with countless pillows and tulle hanging around the bed frame. I was so distracted by the aesthetic shift towards an ornate softness that I missed the door closing behind me.

The sound of water could faintly be picked up and I continued on to find a small pool near the center of the room. It trailed down marble and was contained by river rocks that formed a path. I followed until it made a tiny waterfall over the balcony. Henri was sitting at a table off to the side. "Your room is beautiful."

A soft smile briefly crossed his lips, I understood the appeal of suitors at least wanting to visit. "Thank you."

"So, I may not be an expert on love and magic, but I had some thoughts."

Henri nodded for me to sit across from him. I pulled out a wood chair. Whatever I had planned to say was lost as I caught his eyes. The iris was a slit, instead of perfectly round, surrounded by endless specks of yellow and black. "How'd they change?"

It took him a second to follow. "My eyes? It's the magic. Yours do it to."

"Like that?"

He shook his head once. "No. They catch the light like an animal. Suppose magic is in both our natures."

I leaned back in my seat trying to figure out this mysterious man.

"Do you know who you are now?" he asked, seemingly trying to do the same.

"No."

"Why?"

"I lost my memories."

The truth went seemingly ignored as he poured me a cup of tea. "There's something queer about you."

"Is that why you are demanding we stay? In order to court me?" I realized he hadn't meant it as an insult a moment too late. After my tongue had gotten the best of me.

Henri held his hurt well; fingers laced around his own teacup. A cold front blew in from the open balcony. "I have never, and would never, demand that from someone. I said no because you broke the salt ring. I'm not even sure how. I've never seen someone do so without physically touching it. Channeling all of that. Can be..." He searched for a word. "Triggering. Even with practice, it can be overwhelming, but you know the limits your body can take. I wanted to make sure you were okay first."

I ran a hand through my long hair. "No holding out for true love's kiss then?"

Blessedly he smiled, taking the joke as lighthearted as I had hoped. "Maybe we should practice just to be safe."

I laughed to keep from being actually tempted. "You don't really want a suitor, do you?"

"It's what I want more than anything. But I think everyone tells my story the way they see it. Find it useful for whatever their wants are. As one of the nine, it's expected of me to find a princess. There's plenty I want in life. Money. Power. Champagne. If pretending I'm playing their game, buys me the time to live by my own rules. Well, I can live with that."

My tea sat untouched, and I took a sip in hopes it would give me more courage. "Can you actually turn into a frog?"

"Stars, no. Transmutation is very costly magic. The mirrors show both literal and figurative truths."

"Do you..." I licked my lips, hoping for a yes on this question more than anything I could have asked. "Do you know me?"

"No. I'm sorry to say I haven't met you before, Malcolm Wolf."

The name uttered together made a voice echo in my head. "Lieutenant," I added to his confusion. "It's one of the few things I remember. She… Red was taunting me saying I could be her Lieutenant."

"Red Riding Hood?"

I nodded. "You know her?"

"Know of. Grew up in these parts. She now serves as the Queen's right hand. Oh… that's what happened to her."

The Prince sat in front of me, but I also saw her face. A moment of fear I never thought possible from her.

"Malcolm. Hey, Mal." His hand reached out to touch my arm. "Stay here."

"Sorry, what did you say?" Maybe there was an unspoken likeness between us because his touch was grounding.

"You didn't lose your memories, as if they were misplaced like a set of marbles. I think you traded them for something."

"In a battle."

He nodded, probably trying to encourage. The weight of his gaze, waiting for more was frustrating because I had nothing again, despite any reassurance. Prince Henri saw that too. "Don't worry about it."

"Why not? I barely know where I ever am. When I dream everything feels in my control, but when I'm awake nothing changes despite how much thought I put into it."

"You should be able to cast without your memories. Start with something small."

"Like what?"

Henri glanced down to my cup. "Your tea is getting cold."

The Prince went to bed before I figured it out. I was racing against the sun to get my drink to be anything other than room temperature. I was tempted to crawl under the covers with him because the night's warmth bled out giving way to a chill. I would have cursed the cold, but it was the easiest excuse for my failure. I made Sophie's doll spin. Was it just a toy for mage children? Why had this been so much harder?

I woke up, head resting on my arm on the table. Teacup still sitting there. If dreams were easier for me, maybe—I stuck a finger in the cup. Cold.

Damn it.

There was a short laugh behind me. Henri was spread out on a chaise lounge studying me over the book in his hand. "It's a shame all the good men are taken. You're pretty cute."

"Yeah?" It was too early in the morning for this conversation, and the well of emotions around it. "You are going to regret saying that if Robin isn't my boyfriend."

"Probably." He rubbed the back of his neck. "To be clear, I asked the mirrors to show me love. It is clear that someone in that forest cares about you enough to fight to get you back."

I waved his comment off, placing my head into my hands. "I don't even know if Sherwood Forest is a real place. Maybe I made it up. Or it's an inside secret name."

Henri's book closed, and as he walked over, I thought I might die of embarrassment before he put a far too comforting hand on my shoulder. "Don't worry. I've heard of it before. You aren't as lost in this world as you fear."

Chapter Six

The fact that Jonathan and Sophie were still traveling with me was something I had not overlooked, nor did I understand. If this had been for a grand reward, his only chance might be a favor from a woman who gave none. Jonathan didn't volunteer a new answer, and the fact that I didn't want to be alone, held my tongue as to why they hadn't turned back.

We rode with the destination of Sherwood in mind. The map showed plenty of forests, but none of them where labeled. Some were just patches of trees, another winded around a whole corner.

Our stomachs had been growling for hours before we gave up for the day and decided to make a stew from meager leftovers. The meal gave me something important to focus on.

Jonathan stared at the horizon. "I hate to suggest it, but we should camp here. A storm is coming and if one of our horses gets injured it will be a tragedy on multiple fronts."

"Yeah, alright."

Sophie plopped down exactly where she was, kicking up a cloud of dust with her lack of ceremony. When I laughed at her, she stuck out her tongue. I very maturely returned the gesture.

After dishing out equal portions for Jonathan, and Sophie, then cleaning while they ate so I didn't ruin the small pot we had to make everything in, I finally sat down myself to eat.

"Where's Sophie?"

"She just got her…" I looked over to where she had been and realized how past tense that was. Her bowl was sitting there, half finished. But she was gone.

Jonathan eyed the horizon again. Clear of people, but not of storm clouds. It only took him a second to debate running into the forest to try to find her before she went too far. I stared down at my warm bowl of food, only for a second, before he yelled for me to join him. Deeply hating that he was right.

I grabbed my bag and ran into the forest to catch up with them both. It's possible that Sophie's small frame made the fallen trees and thick brush easier to get through. We almost had to chop our way through to a path. After circling around the same clearing two or three times I stopped to catch my bearings.

"Do you have anything in that bag to help?" Jonathan asked. I barely pulled out the first thing, a rope, before he went on. "Toss that. We aren't going to need it."

Ignoring him, I looped it over my hand so I could reach the other stuff better. He was upset and worried, while I was starving, adding more words into the mix wouldn't help anyone. I found a hard roll of bread I was going to attempt to soften in the stew. "Here, make breadcrumbs so at least we don't get lost."

We made slower time but stopped retracing our steps. Only then after making our own path, did we find one that no way a child could miss. A gingerbread cabin with candy wafer shingles stood in front of us. Swirled peppermint tiles lead up to the front door, which had a matching, but broken, handle.

"Do you see—"

Jonathan started and I grabbed his shirt pulling him back against a tree with me. Holding a finger to my mouth before trying to get another look.

An aged woman looked over the mess at her door mat. "Take, take, take. Kids never ask these days," she mumbled to herself as she poured something over the broken pieces on the ground.

Her arms lifted and the bits floated up. Hands slammed together and the pieces snapped back in place.

"What is she?" Jonathan whispered.

Mouthing the answer didn't help since he didn't know what word I was saying. When the woman went back inside, he started to move again.

I caught his arm. "You can't just storm in there. She might turn you into a gummy bear or something."

He pulled away. "I don't care. My sister could be in there."

"Be smart about this." He waited, for half a second. Without any real patience, I had no time to come up with an actual plan. "Fine, go. I'll come in as a distraction shortly after so you two can run out."

He went for the tactic of just walking up to the door and knocking. I hid behind a tree, making sure I couldn't be seen.

"I believe you have someone important to me," he

declared, and I heard the candy door close again before I ventured a look.

After crawling around to a side window, I stayed crouched hoping no one could see me this low. Inside was a large stove with a bubbling cast iron cauldron.

"I do love when siblings come to dinner," the old woman said. From this angle I couldn't see anymore, but least that confirmed things. A weapon was needed. The best I found was a giant gumdrop that turned hard as a rock after being left outside. If only Jonathan would come out and explain the candy cottage was sweetly not evil. Any second now...

When that didn't happen, I backed up a bit and hurled the gumdrop through the window. It shattered and I climbed in after. Glass crunching under me as I landed. "Hope I'm not late for dinner."

The mage had already turned to the window, her eyes lifting to me as Jonathan ran towards Sophie. "Don't you look sweet," she said ignoring them for a moment as Jonathan worked to untie his sister from the leg of an end table.

A crackling ball of light brought my attention to the mage. Its existence dimmed the fire and flickered in tune with it. She whipped some of the flames towards me.

"Stop!" I brought my arm up reflexively to protect my face. The colors danced around my fingers. Moving just like Prince Henri's smoke had innately followed my control.

"Go." Unsure of who I was even talking to. Everyone. My friends to flee. The old mage. Magic that waited for another order. The first listened. The second stared. The third gathered more from the fireplace until my fingers flexed back to hold its weight.

"How... what are you?" The mage asked. She stared

before fear took over and cowered behind her dining table.

A smirk tugged at a corner of my mouth. "Hungrier than you."

Finding my way back was easier with the breadcrumbs we left, and the still burning fire behind me. It mostly glowed a red hue but there were times were a bit of magic left in the house would spark off adding shades of green and blue. Sure, I didn't have to burn her whole house down. But it didn't feel responsible to leave a cannibal that lured kids in either. Jonathan and Sophie were too far ahead to add any judgement they might have.

I caught up with them at the nearest edge of the forest. Even though it was off the breadcrumb trail. Jonathan had already started scolding Sophie when I approached.

"There you are," he sighed in relief before turning back to Sophie. "What were you thinking? Why did you leave camp?"

Her hands fidgeted. Knowing she did wrong, but also just wanting to be out of trouble as fast as possible. "There was this glow in the trees. I figured they were fairies like mom talked about. After my wish, I thought they appeared to make it come true."

"What wish?" Jonathan asked harshly.

Ah, shit.

I started to wander off, half hoping to find my stew when I heard Sophie start sniffling. Keep walking, Mal, I told myself. But couldn't leave her crying like that. "She wanted to see something your parents had."

"What?" He looked up at me, finally appearing as sad and worried as he actually felt before turning to his sister with a much softer expression. "Really Soph?"

She nodded and sniffled again. Jonathan wiped her tears and softly spoke that next time she had to save such sights for the both of them.

I walked ahead to give them some privacy. Never finding my dinner but found myself oddly not hungry anymore.

After an hour of walking slowly, Sophie moved ahead of me. Suddenly stopping to check for her brother's approval. "That's perfect, thank you."

"Everything okay?" I asked.

He nodded. "It is now. I don't know what you did but thank you."

"Sure thing." Did he want to know what happened? The burning building came back to me and I decided he didn't. "Jonathan, I got to ask. Why are you still on this quest? It's clearly not safe for Sophie, and there's probably no rewards to reap."

He crossed his arms, walking a bit further before even attempting to put words to an answer. "Sophie is too young to remember our parents. They are nothing but stories to her. To me? Our house, that city, even the ocean itself. It reminds me of nothing but them. I stayed put because it was a life for her. But I was being smothered by my memories there. You not having any, the Queen going missing. It felt like a sign. Maybe it was all just weak justification."

I placed a hand on his arm, remembering how someone being there helped me. A weak smile followed, hoping to be reassuring. "Good of a reason as any."

"Thanks." He put a hand over mine, tapping it before meeting back up with his sister.

I was happy to have him give me a moment because I realized with a growing annoyance that not only had we separated ourselves from some of the supplies. But the horses.

Since we had left the forest at a different spot, we had no way of knowing which direction they were. Hopefully, their own wishes included freedom.

Chapter Seven

Hope kept me moving. Signs of life. Curiosity powering my muscles to travel over a large stone bridge. This should mean people, supplies, news maybe.

As the sun rose, so did music. "What even is that? A violin?" I laughed to myself trying to track down the sound. Only stopping when Jonathan called my name a bit distantly.

"No one is allowed to run off anymore," Jonathan said, as him and Sophie caught up.

"You hear that, right? It's beautiful."

"Exactly what I'm worried about."

"If you let me find it, I promise I'll never hold losing the horses against you."

"That—" He took a moment to pull in his anger, while Sophie did her best seen and not heard impression. "Fine, deal."

We walked longer than I think any of us intended. The

song had to be enchanted because its sound carried unnaturally well through the town. I did a double take any time a villager broke from their daily routine to look our way swearing there must be an instrument in their hands. Compared to other places we visited this one was bustling with bakers working alongside families that lived by. Each knitted close to one another and the land they tended.

They heard the music too. Some seemed to have learned to ignore it, but others swayed along as they went about their lives.

On the outskirts, looking over the city next to the bay were the remains of an impossibly large tree that once stood. Now its countless rings made for a stage. A man with curling horns played the violin. We hadn't seen a single Card, but the figure was a regal as any royal we've met.

The music echoed differently here. Revibrated deeper in my bones despite the open-air stage. It felt like an altar too holy to touch so I slowed to a stop on the top stair.

"Um, excuse me. Sir?" Jonathan called to the figure playing.

The man turned, bow stopping the song mid-note to look at us. "Dispel your magic."

"We aren't doing any." Johnathan tried to reassure, but the Beast was now looking past him and Sophie completely. To me.

"I'm not doing…" After looking around I realized I couldn't truthfully finish my sentence. My shadow was stretching out past where the sun would have it. Growing longer than I've ever seen.

"If you don't," the Beast continued, horns giving an extra width to a man already larger than us, making the instrument look even more delicate in his hands, "you are going to end up summoning a creature."

Attempts to step away didn't help given that the shadow was practically sown on to my feet. My fear, or his scorn, won out before any more useless attempts on my part.

"Is your magic truly triggered by emotion?"

The pity only flared my temper, proving his theory as the shadow's shape grew darker. "Could you just help me?"

"The place is warded against the Queen's corruption. It's your demon." The Beast lifted his violin to play once more.

Sophie threw herself at him. Her weight throwing him a step off balance, and not much more. "No, you listen! He's our friend."

If she had any other nice things to say about me, I didn't get the chance to hear them as my shadow started to crawl up my legs before engulfing me.

A girl ran through the forest, looking behind her every few steps. Each time she stole a glance, a wolf vanished from sight. Weaving between the trees for cover as if it were a game to the creature.

Her foot caught on a fallen branch. Wicker basket sent flying, before landing a short distance in front of her. With a scramble up she managed to grab the basket, but surely the animal would prey on her delay.

Then, nothing. Not a soul in sight.

Getting to a cottage was a blur of fear. And when she entered everything was covered in dust. Her hand wiped clean a silver mirror to show a woman reading the arched embossed words. "Elle avoit vû le loup."

"Heard you were looking for me," I said, stepping out from a direction I hadn't been watching from. Perspective molding to this new position instead. Adorned in the black and gold uniform that otherwise matched the Riders.

"Do you chase all your future allies through the forest?"

I grunted a reply. Bored of her games already and tugged my uniform down staring at what looked like a paw print on my tunic. "The Treaty of the Nine put a leash on us both. What is it you called me for?"

"Sit." The woman removed her cape, placing it on the back of the chair of where she wanted me.

I did as she asked. Unable to not. This wasn't right.

"A month from now the Queen will visit her spring house," Red said as she leaned over to grab a brush. "I will set up a time for you to meet then. With our groups combined power we can bring about change."

The refection in this pure silver mirror was tarnished and without detail. She brushed my hair back, holding strands as she tied it up with a red ribbon. Pieces not quite long enough fell forward onto my face. "Soon you'll be ready."

"This... this isn't what happened."

Red gave no sign she heard what was said. Panic gripped me as she leaned in over my shoulder. Lips grazing my ear before she spoke. "You shall be the Queen of Hearts' first club. A Card so violent, angry, and senseless that compared to you, no one will question their new Red Queen."

A girl ran through the trees, looking behind her every few steps. With every stolen glance, a wolf vanished from sight. Weaving between anything in its path as if it were a contest.

"No," the animal wined.

Her foot caught on a fallen branch. Basket flying, landing a short distance in front of her. With a scramble she managed to grab it, but surely the animal would seize on any chance.

She brushed my hair back, holding stray strands as she tied it up with a ribbon.

"Robin... he'll come for me." My voice only a whimper.

She gave no sign she heard what was said. Panic crashed over me again as she leaned in over my shoulder. "Don't cry, Wolf."

I ran through the forest, looking behind every few steps. Each time to steal a glance of red vanishing from sight. Weaving between the trees for cover as if being played with.

My foot caught on a fallen branch. I fell into my shadow as if it could hide me from all harm and be invisible within its shape.

There was weight on my side. When I refused to move, it moved. A slobber coated my face. "Okay, you found me, stop."

"Mal! Mal, wake up."

I stared at a wolf sitting in front of me. One that could talk? "Wait... Sophie?"

The wolf moved to lick my face again. This time when I opened my eyes, I was on the Beast's stage. With Sophie, and over a hundred pounds of canine sitting inches from my face.

Looking up barely helped put any of the pieces together. The antlers betrayed, or maybe better expressed the slight surprise of a man I first saw only moments before passing out. "I need someone to tell me what the hell just happened."

"I'm sorry. My name is Adam, I protect this town. What I hadn't accounted for was someone corrupted by magic like you are." He held his hand out, and I took it simply happy for the chance to just stand again.

"I knew it. Cursed."

"No, more..." He struggled to find the right word. "Scarred. I hadn't believed your friends that you weren't one of the Queen's men. Until the shadow creature you summoned fed off your own nightmares."

"Cursed." Maybe if I repeated myself, he'd believe me.

"You are extremely powerful. But poisoned. The connection between you and magic itself is tainted. It's just anger and fear now."

The temptation to yell at him to listen to me was tempered by Jonathan standing at a distance. He was looking at me differently. Figures, turning into a shadow creature for a moment could do that to some people.

Unable to hold out waiting for him to catch my eye any longer, I turned back to Adam. "How'd you get the nightmare to stop?"

"The music was only meant to have meaning for those who need it. This place is a refuge. Those in need of a safe place or animals who are wounded. It's meant to feed the soul. Heal." It seemed like another apology was coming, but he reigned it back in maybe realizing he hadn't answered my question. "This is a familiar. It helps ground memories that overflow."

I reached out still doubting the wolf was a living thing. The animal closed the gap, tucking his usual height under my hand ready for a pet. Definitely too attentive to be a wild animal.

"He'll serve you. Protect you. Fight with you. Channel your magic as you relearn it. Please consider his service my apologies for the harm caused."

"Is Mal going to be okay now?" The question unexpectedly came from Jonathan. I wanted to declare that a win and be done, but Adam's unsure grimace made my new wolf growl a little.

Unafraid of the animal himself, Adam just gave it a glance before explaining. "I can't say for sure because I don't know it's true origins. But what happened was because there was a spell attached to you, that is now broken."

"Look here," Jonathan said, angrier than I ever heard. "Answer the question. Is Mal okay?"

Certainly felt better knowing my only friends didn't hate me. But I didn't add to the discussion because I too wanted the answer.

"I'm being honest with you. I don't know. Better than before probably." He looked over to me. "What was wrong?"

"I couldn't remember anything." The realization that I now could was like the whole world shifted, while nothing changed. That's why I knew being Red's Card wasn't real. There were actual memories to compare it against. "Shit. I remember everything."

Chapter Eight

My memories were a field ready for harvest. We had moved to Adam's farmhouse, and sat around his dining table as if we were equals. Despite the nagging feeling that this Adam was also a Prince of Heart. A group of royals named in half ode, half concession to the Hart family. Only notable public figure, Cassandra Hart. Better known as the Queen, and ruler of Wonderland.

Believe it or not, getting exactly what you wanted isn't all sunshine and glitter. Now I was prone to blurting out long explanations to anyone who didn't understand the politics of the nine united kingdoms. Every thought felt blown apart. If prompted I could pick out the related bit of knowledge. Given I had known in the first place.

"Let me see if I can get this straight," Adam said, and I resisted the urge to correct him for the sake of a joke. "Robin and his merry men were going to work with Red Riding Hood."

"Ava."

The confused shake of his head caused hair to fall over

his horns. "We will get back to that part in a moment. Follow me here. The plan was to work with her, both advocating for the people by asking the Queen to relinquish some power."

"Right. But she made it out to look like we just were a gang of thieves who wanted to undermine her authority." That part might have been true but wasn't true in a sense either.

Jonathan leaned in trying to strategize with us. Only Sophie had quit in favor of a nap. I loved it all. Made losing everything feel worth it. It had changed the world. Except there was also a big problem. If the spell on Ava that was tied to me had broken, then all my suffering happened for nothing. Wait—Jonathan had asked a question.

"Isn't there a belief that if you know someone's true name you have power over them? Can you do anything with that knowledge? See if someone's alive or send them a message?"

My familiar shook his head for me. Either extremely tuned in or had an itch. I gave him a pat either way. "You need more than that to really influence anyone. The connection between you and the person has to be extraordinarily strong."

"What about Robin?"

That was a piece of me I hadn't wanted to touch. Largely because of how much I felt was still missing. Not for lack of desire on my part. Being in love with your best friend since childhood was great in ways. But also had for a deep always present want for more, more, an unending deep hunger for more.

My new wolf friend laid his head on my knee grounding me back to this moment.

Adam leaned back in his chair considering everything for

a silent minute or so. "Ava is a palindrome."

When neither of us seemed to understand, he went on. "It loops. Like your nightmare was. The Rider's power as an organization was always that they were the same corrupt system just like the Cards had been. What gave them an opportunity was they were different by one. Women who could claim solidarity with the Queen, in ways her father's Cards never could."

The growing feeling that Robin and I had been used as pawns settled into my bones with a cold chill. Everyone I knew was just a plaything in a silent smiling battle to seize power. She probably even preferred to be "Little Red Riding Hood" versus her actual name. Made her seem timid. Small. Compared to me, the big bad ruiner of things she wanted.

The wolf resting on my legs, picked his head up. He pawed at me then looked over to the door to the backyard.

I followed where he was focusing, trying to figure out what he was attempting to say. "I think this semi-wild animal needs to go outside. You two go on."

The wolf did seem happier out here. Running around the backyard with a playfulness that made me smile. The scent of the trees also felt a little like home. I told myself I'd come back inside once I thought of a name for the creature.

Within the hour, I'd given up on both things. Content in doing and thinking about nothing at all. Only to be convinced to simply watch the sunset, even after the animal headed inside himself.

If Adam liked men, I was never going to leave. The view of the stars from his farm was to die for. I thought nothing could top how bright they got within the darkness of a forest. What I hadn't anticipated for was the clear skies of this region. Plus, the guy gave me my very own magical service dog. Definitely a keeper for whatever beauty caught his eye.

In truth, the desire to stay here wasn't very deep. I wanted to see my best friend again. Couldn't let him kill someone because we had lost each other. Flung apart by careless magic all because I thought turning Ava to stone would result in less bloodshed.

Maybe I was right on that front. Wasn't sure if I was on others.

The sliding door opened and out trotted Jonathan and my new wolf. "We wanted to check on you."

That was a lie. And I was fairly sure this familiar could get a read of me from a mile away. Connected on a level that was hard to cut without a stronger rebuff. But it was a beautiful lie. "Thanks."

We shared the quiet night together for a moment before Jonathan's nervous shifting let me know something else was on his mind. "I'd like to see this through with you. If you don't find me and Sophie too plain. I want to see you safely home, wherever that really is. Finish something that matters even if it isn't finding the Queen."

"Oh, we'll find her."

"Yeah?"

I nodded. "Certain of it." My actions rippled through the world changing it forever already. "I can't promise it's safe. It's chewed me up and spit me out at least once."

Jonathan looked at the town, dimly visible with a nearly new moon. "Did I ever tell you how my parents died?"

I shook my head.

"They were merchants for years. Away on travel for weeks at a time. They said it was no life for a kid, so I ended up staying at my aunts as soon as I could walk really. Then my mom got pregnant again. Two children left behind was their limit, I guess. They gave up the life they had, all the dangerous and wonderous places they knew for peace on the beach. Never having to transport anything more than the length of the docks. One night there was a storm. Every abled person shipped out to rescue a big vessel. Most of the crew was saved. But a lifeboat manned by my father was lost. My mother faded away after that. Both gone before Sophie was old enough to take care of herself. I told her the stories that they left me with. The thing that killed them, Mal," he said, finally turning to look over at me, "was holding still. If something happens to us, I don't want it to be an act of nature. Good or bad it should be from our choices."

Adam joined us on the now crowded patio. Jonathan cleared his throat, covering he was saying anything at all let alone a confession like that. "The tents are ready for you."

Mere seconds later, it was just the two of us again. "About what you said," I prompted before he turned in for the night. "It was really powerful. Far more self-determined than most people are in this world."

"I think you're a good person." Jonathan smiled. "No matter what anyone ends up saying about you."

"Thanks?" I laughed. "You going to help me find where these tents are, so I don't wander around?"

"Sure thing." We stepped inside and I was instantly tackled by sixty pounds of pre-teen. Despite the late time, Sophie was very much awake now.

"Where we are staying looks so cool. Come on, come on." She took my hand and decided to drag me through the house and out the front door.

They were located a short walk from the farm, but definitely interesting looking. Imagination had me picturing a couple of sticks tied together with a tarp thrown over it. Instead, they were circular cloth yurts. Maybe half a dozen of them in the area counting at a glance.

Jonathan and Sophie said their goodnights and ducked into one. Only once inside my own did I notice the circular hole in the roof, positioned above a lit camping stove. It burned just hot and bright enough that I could see around the single room and set out anything for sleeping. This time, I was able to use my wolf as a pillow. Something equally as wonderful as it was strange.

"What star do you think is right there?" I stared up at the tiny bit of starlight that was getting in. I couldn't make out any constellation, but it might be the north star. "What about Polaris? That's a fairly good one."

The wolf let out a huff of air before stretching his back feet out. He seemed content enough with that name. To do list: done.

In the morning, no food was prepared so I sat outside my yurt wondering if familiars could also be used as hunting dogs.

Sophie walked up to me with a bouquet of weeds. The only flowering thing she held out was yellow dandelions. "Can you make food with this?"

"Uh." Polaris let out a big huff and put his head on the ground. I smiled, thinking he also wanted to catch something. "Where's your brother, Soph?"

"He's still sleeping. We were up late, and I thought it would be nice to have a meal ready when he woke up. So, can we use these?" She held the weeds out to me again.

"Least you didn't bring me the fluffy bits."

"Those are for wishes, silly."

Polaris and I stood up as one. "You're a smart kid. Let's go work on that breakfast idea of yours." In the morning light, a shared area between all the tents could be seen. It was a slightly dug out space with an iron skillet hanging off it. The kettle would work for boiling water, and the pan could be used for bacon or to toast bread if any more could be found.

"My mom would make these into a salad," Sophie said softly.

I turned to look at her. She was just staring at the weeds. "Is that what you want to make?"

"No." She looked up at me. "What do you think we should do?"

"How about tea and maybe we can find a fishing pole since this camp site is decently stocked."

"Okay! I'll go find one." Sophie barely finished talking before she ran off around a different yurt to go look. I glanced over to where Jonathan was sleeping figuring it was okay if he didn't know.

I dipped the kettle into the water and started a fire to heat it. A bush rustled out of time with the wind catching both my and Polaris' attention. "Go get it."

The wolf was off with a bolt. Jumping over the bushes and out of sight. A few seconds of stillness later he walked around with a still alive rabbit carefully between his teeth.

"You can hunt!"

There was a scream behind me, and I turned to see Sophie standing there in horror. "You can't kill that little animal!"

I hung my head, not knowing why we could torture fish, but not eat other meat. Must be the blood. "Drop him, boy."

The wolf's jaw opened an inch and the animal fell out of his mouth. It didn't move for a moment, probably in shock, but with a little growl the rabbit came to its senses and bolted.

Sophie approached, carefully from my side suddenly less sure about my new pet. She had found a fishing pole, but we hadn't caught anything by time Jonathan was up.

"Sorry to make you watch Sophie all morning," he said, with his hands wrapped around the warm tea I managed to finish. "You're good with kids. Did you have any siblings growing up?"

I decided to not fill him in on almost making Sophie cry via hunting prey and focused on the latter. Memories of a group of boys chasing each other around and climbing trees came to me. None of us were actually related, more so all lost boys grouped together. "No, but kids just like to be kids. It's easy when you aren't a parent because all you have to do is not get in the way when they are excited."

Jonathan laughed a little. "Guess that's true."

"Are you sure you want to carry on with me?"

"I told you last night..." His eyes suddenly looked so serious. Their stunning green coloring made me just want to agree to whatever he said. I wanted to be capable of shouting: Sure, join me! I'll keep you away from any harm.

But in truth... "It's dangerous. You might not be safe."

"I told you—"

"I know." My hand raised to hold back any more of his words. "Just needed to make sure you had slept on it first."

"Do you know where we should go next?"

I finished my tea and stood before finally answering. "I know how we might find out, but I'm not sure the idea is going to work."

Part Two: All The Queen's Men
Chapter Nine

Confidence had led us, for the second time in two days, towards the musical creature playing a song over the city.

One of his notes went sour when I told him of my plan. "You want me to summon the Queen's Cards. Here?"

"Yes." Our eyes locked. A challenge for the other to back down. "Tell me Prince Adam, why are there no Cards around in the first place?"

He glanced away, giving a low gravelly scoff. "They were asked to leave." The tone told me exactly how they were made to stay away. By force. The Beast's temperament yielded. "I have no real desire to control them, so if I bring any here for you to try to get information from, they'll likely end up hostile. You think you can handle that?"

I smirked. "Just don't make your song too compelling."

He picked his violin up and took a deep breath before he started to play. The song started off slow, building up with a repetition that seemed to pick up another instrument each time. Within half a minute it was a battle cry calling out to reach the nearest Cards.

The notes made the hair on my arms rise. Any man with a connection to a magical current would be drawn here.

Within minutes familiar suited guards appeared. I could hear the questions the Beast asked them in the back of my head. "Where did you come from? Is the Queen alive?"

I stood where I had passed out just the day before, with my palms angled towards the ground. Glimmering shadows poured from my hands. Shifting to make a dome around the old tree stump before spreading through the city, walling off the Cards from the citizens. The summoned men were funneled towards us.

One ascended the steps, forced to stop a stair below. He looked at the Beast as if there was nothing out of the ordinary about this at all. Music calling to him, much like the Queen's own control. "We were stationed outside Rapunzel's tower."

A different guard stopped another step lower, now speaking in unison. "The Queen lives. We still feel her."

Another spoke, "Our Queen wouldn't have been caught if it hadn't been her plan."

The odd group didn't behave like normal soldiers under a chain of command. They were bewitched, responding like a single loyal man.

The Card in front hit against the shield. Face skewing with annoyance that a song in his head called forward, forward, forward but there was no more ground to comply.

"Have you had contact with her recently?" The Beast asked, the notes changing with another question: "Where is she?"

"We won't let you find her first. The disloyal must be

punished," the Cards said in tandem. They pulled weapons, a few squeezing together on the top step to break my protection spell.

I could feel my control slip as their sense did. The tiptoeing around them, prince after prince who only cared about their wishes, not the world itself.

There was a growl at my side. Polaris baring his teeth at a Card outside the bubble. I refused to cave. Looking away from them to my own hands. Runes appeared. Floating around my wrists. Sharp shapes and broken letters. They shined bright in a pulse with the Card's attempts.

Something slick ran down from my nose. Without thinking, I moved a hand to wipe it away, finding drops of blood on my fingers. Why did I always forget that protecting people was always a harder magic? It flowed all over the city spreading me out thin even with the support animal.

I screamed at them, "Answer him!"

"You are nothing. Worse than vermin."

Maybe I should have been concerned that I heard them thinking that, rather than actually saying it to my face. But the Beast started to sing. Strong and clear despite being in a language I couldn't pick the words out from.

I pulled a wispy shadow out of the air, and magic crackled within the shape. Rather than doubting myself, the magic sang along to the Beast's tale. Telling of lost things returned, and victory.

My victory.

With a snap of my fingers the protective dome shattered into thousands of shimmering shards, slowly turning in unison before flying towards the Cards. Anywhere. Everywhere they were within the city.

They fell. Some tumbling down the stairs. Their outfits

tarnished with ash. The Beast stepped ahead, rushing down to check the pulse of the first he could reach.

"That was…" Jonathan said.

"Effortless." Hadn't I been the man who couldn't warm tea? I felt nearly the same as before, but that didn't stop Jonathan's expression from changing. Maybe he just realized that his vision of a happy ending didn't match up with my powers.

Polaris moved from me and wandered over to Sophie. I feared she'd be afraid of both of us now, but puppy eyes and tail wags worked to gain pets of approval. "Thank you for helping us stay safe."

"These men are alive," Adam said, stepping back up to join us. "It will take a bit of work to sort which of them are just rotten, and those who are now free. They came from Rapunzel's tower. That is where you should go next."

"Come with us," Jonathan added.

Adam shook his head. "You'll be just as safe with Malcolm. My music is an amplifier, and my people will need help cleaning up." He rubbed his fingers together examining the soot there.

Unsure if I wanted his opinion, I interrupted. "Is it true that she has a chess board that shows those in power?"

He nodded. "Whatever your next move becomes, it needs to take in the whole picture first. She's protected, but she may talk to you. Just because these men were near her, they still were completely under the Queen's control. I think she's getting desperate. Cards normally have more of a mind of their own."

As if to either agree or disagree, one of the Card's groaned as he woke up.

"Go. Travel straight to the North. Shouldn't take you

more than a day on foot."

The walk to Rapunzel's tower was quiet. Maybe halfway through Sophie started complaining about her feet hurting and convinced Jonathan to give her a piggyback ride. I think she just wanted a better view from his shoulders of the grass plain. After forest and seaside villages tucked against cliffs this looked endless.

When a tower dotted the horizon, Jonathan broke the silence. "What do you know about Rapunzel?"

I hadn't ever seen her, but it was a story that was told to anyone curious about the Royals of Heart. "Fearing the world so, her father locked her away from it all. Every day when he came to visit, she'd complain to him saying she couldn't see anything from where she was. So, he enchanted a chess board. Each piece represented a group. Coveted by anyone looking to go to battle because it will tell you the movements of others."

Sophie winkled her nose. "That doesn't sound like a fun game."

"No. No, it's not."

"Wait," Jonathan said. "I was told that her mother was ill. And her father traded his first born for a cure. It saved his wife's life, but they never were able to raise their daughter because she was locked too high away from them. That's wrong?"

All I could do is shrug. Truth was one thing. Story was another. A tale could completely change when given context. Or truth utterly hidden if certain details were removed.

Whatever Cards had been camping out here, had been magically pulled away. Their supplies littered the meadow. Once we were close enough to stare up from the base of the tower, there didn't seem to be any handholds to climb up. I was trying to think of a magical solution when something was thrown out of the window.

We all drew back expecting an attack of some sort, but a piece of wood attached to a rope hung down. The building had its own pulley system. "Looks like an invite to me." I glanced up, not seeing anyone at the other end. "I'll go first."

Up, and up, and up I was pulled. Holding onto the rope as the height became dizzying. A woman with strikingly golden hair offered a hand, and I took it because falling here was not an option.

Without my weight the platform lowered slightly. The room was round. Sectioned off in both sunken and raised areas. Her braid reached to the middle of the room and I followed it back up to her face. Then behind her to the window where a jeweled dagger sat. "If you have a quarrel, it should be with me, not them."

She paused and leaned to look out the window and below. "I had only expected you. They aren't more wolves, are they?"

"They are friends."

Rapunzel nodded, but didn't look like she actually understood the word I said. She grabbed the knife and moved away. "You can help them up."

Once Jonathan and Sophie were safely inside, I turned to her again, her gaze still studying us. She seemed mostly interested in Sophie who commented on how fun this tower was. I grew anxious over the fact that the actual wolf was sitting alone on the ground level. The platform had been too small for him to sit on. Add in the lack of thumbs to hold on and it seemed like a disaster waiting to happen.

"How did you know who I am? Or that I was coming?"

A tremor rippled through her fingers. "My chess board showed me."

"I'm a piece on it?"

Jonathan shot me a look, clearly less surprised. "Is the Queen okay? We are looking for her."

"Of course." Her eyes narrowed. "You can't have it."

"We don't want to take your things," Sophie reassured. "Or you. If you were worried. You seem nice."

"Oh." The tension in her shoulders released. "Okay. I'll show you."

For a moment, I thought she had just meant Sophie, but she carefully waited and watched for us all to walk in front of her. Sitting on a table in the back of the room was a large model of the area. Spaces with few details had a checkered pattern as a base. I could spot the fishing town along the shore, Prince Phillip's castle. Beast's town. And here, where a pawn sat on top of the tower.

"Is that me?"

"Rather silly to include myself. I always know where I am," she joked. Her light laugh ended short when I didn't join in on it.

"What are the others?" Sophie asked. Her fingers were just over the edge as if she wanted to pick up one of the dozen or so pieces. She pointed towards an elk figure. "Oh! That one is the Beast, isn't it?"

"It is." She smiled and leaned down to be on Sophie's level. "This was a gift from my father. It usually includes the others of Heart. But sometimes I'll spot a knight or pawn moving about."

"The board controls itself?" Jonathan asked. A small frog glided over a square as if asked to prove it.

Rapunzel nodded. "These days most only move a few squares around their castles. While the Queen normally travels between her houses along with the seasons."

"Where is Robin?"

"I... who?"

Jonathan gave me another look that in my frustration I couldn't read. "Which one is the Queen?"

The Princess hesitated and glanced over at me nervously before looking back at the board. Not even needing a second to check before pointing towards a crowned figure. "You came after it was working again. For a short while I thought the board was broken since she moved off her usual paths. And before that the Rider's leader had stopped moving all together."

"Our fight." Each memory I got back was a crack in the stone. The horse piece was moving again because of my actions.

"That was you?" The fear in Rapunzel's voice started to grate on me. I had done nothing to her. Everyone I ever cared about who fought, wasn't here. I was. As a pawn.

"An eye for an eye. A Queen for a Queen." I recited back the poem we first saw at Prince Phillip's. "The Queen's movements changed when Robin kidnapped her. This whole mess. All of it was because of me. I gave Robin the motive. By mistake."

Jonathan put a hand on my shoulder. "All we have to do is show them you are fine."

"That doesn't solve the problem." I took a deep breath, placing a finger on Red's piece. "She wants to be rid of the Queen more than anyone else. If she reaches them before we do…"

Jonathan chewed on his thumb nail. "Which do you want to deal with first?"

"Don't deal with any of it!" Rapunzel said, looking at us as if we were rabid. "You see how messed up this world is. And not only do you still want to be a part of it. You mess it up more in your efforts."

"You may be forced to stay here," I growled. "But I care about fixing things."

"Forced?" Rapunzel asked, drawing back in confusion.

"Wait," Sophie said. She picked up the pawn on the tower. "This looks nothing like a wolf. You said you knew it was us."

Rapunzel's nervous hands dropped to her sides, as her cautious gaze turned to the piece in Sophie's hand. "It was shaped like a wolf. Once. I woke up one day, and the original was gone. All I could find was a pawn along the beach on the far side. I assumed it had to be the same because there was no wolf piece. Normally it's in Sherwood. Another reason I thought the whole board was losing its magic."

"I'm not the leader! Why would—" Everyone's sudden stare made me bite down on my tongue.

"You still scare me," Rapunzel said.

If I hadn't already been holding my words back, I might have played up on that fact. Instead, I just backed up like a cornered animal.

"Red would always tell such tales about how angry and mean you are. You run around thinking you are saving the kingdom. But I am witness to it all. I had believed her for a time until the chess board made it clear."

Rapunzel walked around and for the first time took a

step towards me. "You know the real story, don't you? Witnessed more than even I could."

"Shut up."

"I'm not forced to be here, any more than you are." She continued, taking another step. "The world is terrifying and cruel. I choose not to be a part. Seems my story got twisted getting to you, as yours did to mine. Show me the truth."

She filled the distance between us by reaching out a hand. Having nowhere to go, I mirrored her gesture. When the tip of my finger touched hers, a bright light appeared. It glowed like a star. I looked past it, to the shadows dancing in her eyes.

"You put everything you had into your fight with Red. To protect. And she wove together a story that made her look like the victim. And you the Big Bad Wolf." The light dimmed, not just between us, but the whole room. She frowned. "You must still stop her."

"Enough." I ripped my hand away, despite barely touching in the first place. "I gave enough."

"Yes, you did." Rapunzel smiled sadly at me. "Come. I'll help you find what you really want."

We approached the map of everything again, this time she instructed where on the board I should put my hands. She, and Sophie, mirrored me on two other sides. I didn't think that was needed since Rapunzel did not ask Jonathan to complete the fourth.

Nothing happened.

"Close your eyes. Let your heart show you," Rapunzel prompted.

If I was meant to pour my magic into it, this plan wasn't going to work. My connection to it felt like a burnt match after everything I saw tonight.

A felt a glimmer of something and I opened my eyes to a catch the tail end of Rapunzel using twisting magic. A small marble piece appeared in a forested area. The hooded figure had arrows shaped like filigree.

"Robin." *Finally, I found him.*

"That is not Sherwood however," Rapunzel warned.

Jonathan tapped his hand against the board. "Is it safe to go there?"

"No."

I waited for her to go on. Give us something to make our passage possible, but nothing. "I'm going."

The Princess glanced over to Sophie, who was now leaning over the table, using her hands to prop her up. "The child should stay."

"My sister sticks with me."

"It's not safe from here out," Rapunzel warned again.

Jonathan rolled his eyes. "Can you tell the future now too?"

"I'm leaving for that forest at sunrise. You can all have until then to figure out who is and isn't coming with me." I took a step away, heard the start of words from all three people. "Stop and actually weigh the options."

Chapter Ten

I was kicked awake. A single kick rather. With a jolt the world came into focus. Morning light much softer than the start I was given. "Sic him, Polaris."

The wolf I was curled up against for warmth growled at Jonathan. But didn't decide to have him for breakfast since that wasn't what I really wanted. I sat up, rubbing my eyes. "I take it Rapunzel convinced you to let Sophie stay."

"For the time being."

"No need to be an ass about it." I stood, dusting myself off. A quick glance around suggested that Jonathan had just come down, rather than camping here with me for the night. "You don't need to come with me."

Jonathan's brows tightened before he just shook his head. "Let's just get a move on it."

He headed out before I even packed. In a hurry I shoved everything into my bag and caught up. "What's your problem today?"

"The only thing I'm really convinced of is that you aren't

ready to go, but I know I can't stop you."

"Me?" I looked at my familiar, who simply looked back up at me. He seemed fine. I felt fine. "Whatever your issue is you need to knock it off."

Jonathan rolled his eyes. "You don't see yourself when you draw on magic. Is it addicting? With as easily as you seem to revel in it, one could think. So yeah, I'm not thrilled that I either have to leave my sister behind or let you go somewhere unknown and hope your magic holds out."

"I don't need a babysitter."

Polaris trotted out in front of us, leading the way while we argued. Jonathan just gestured towards him as if that were proof I did. "That's a familiar. Mess with me again, and I'm going to have to kick your ass."

"Oh, I'm sure you could." Jonathan huffed. "Look, fine. I'm sorry I had a crash course on everything I'm meant to know about royal drama and I'm unhappy how messed up the world is."

"Kick the messenger while he's down," I sarcastically added, but Jonathan heard it differently.

"Yeah. You did bring this into my life. And I really want to be upset with you for that," he paused, and I resisted the urge to interject. "But it also just makes me respect you more, because you put up with all of it for so long."

My thoughts stalled out. "Thank you?"

"Seriously, Mal. I don't know even the half of it, and it seemed pretty messed up. Magic or not. Shit, maybe being able to do incredible things just made you more of a target."

I didn't know how to take the words being said to me. They were nice, and I largely wanted to hold onto them. After a little bit I just smiled. "Did Rapunzel tell you how far it was?"

"Day and a half."

My enjoyment was waning again. "If I wake up before you tomorrow, I'm kicking you awake." When Jonathan glanced over, I grinned bigger. "To be even. For equality."

He laughed. "Deal."

I knew we were getting in the right general area when trees started appearing and refused to let up.

"Any chance you know more about this dangerous place?"

"Yeah, I took notes." Jonathan started fishing a piece of parchment out of his pocket. "Wait. Why the funny look?"

Feeling embarrassed I shook my head. "Nothing. I uh, didn't realize you were literate."

"Ah, yeah." Jonathan let out a huff. "Learned that was uncommon for 'commoners'. Everyone back home can read and write. We need it to check the shipping manifests and countless other things." He stopped suddenly, both in speech and walking. "Can you?"

"What write?" I shrugged. "Well, enough, I guess. I'm not going to be writing a sonnet anytime soon."

He laughed. "Pretty sure that's a different skill anyways." Jonathan looked up at the trees. They blocked out the sun from sight. All the light around was what had snuck through. "Rapunzel said this place is actually on the edge of Snow White's forest. I neglected to ask if that was a person or a mountain range."

"Person," I laughed.

"How was I to know?"

"I have an unfair advantage seeing as I know her."

His eyes went wide for a second. "Really?"

"Was bound to know someone in this world," I added as I ventured into the woods. Polaris sniffed at the ground before speeding back up to my side. "Next time I do magic beyond my limits I'll try to fling myself to the coast I'm more familiar with. Hey, can I see your notes?"

Jonathan handed them over and I read over everything but found the little map he drew more intriguing. "This is really good. I didn't know so much detail could fit into such a small space. You added Sherwood and everything."

"Thanks." His voice sounded softer than usual, and I glanced over to find him blushing. If he started to like me this close to finding Robin… "Maybe in this newer world you bring about," he continued. "I can write down all the places we've been. Things we've seen. That way the stories don't get forgotten or twisted."

There was a flaw in his beautiful plan. That meant people had to read it first. Saying that to him however was too mean. "I'd like that."

We walked about a half an hour before I stopped again. Took a moment to really study the tree line for movement. Polaris seemed focused there too as he had with the rabbit before.

"What is it?" Jonathan asked softly.

"Something is following us."

"Who?"

I tilted my head. That wasn't quite right. "Maybe more of a what." The feeling of being watched gnawed at me, and I took a step, only to stop again. "I know you're there!"

A large toothy grin appeared above us in the trees. It's smile wide, too wide for the shape of a striped cat that filled in afterwards. "Hello boys. How are you getting on?"

The more I stared up at him the more I realized he wasn't striped at all. The color bands I saw were a rib cage. Nothing but bare bones. This creature was neither living nor dead.

"What is that thing?" Jonathan asked.

The cat purred. "Most ask for directions, you aren't a lost boy, are you? At least not yet." The vibrating sound grew to a laugh. "By the bye," the cat continued. "You should know that dead things still live."

The delighted sound was soon greeted with Polaris' growl. He bared his teeth, more wicked than the cats. I placed a hand on the wolf. "We can see that. Who are you?"

"Who aren't I?" The cat jumped down from the tree. Skeleton breaking into dust as it hit the ground.

Jonathan leapt back. "I don't like it here," he declared as he gave the area a wide berth.

I couldn't disagree there. "Let's find Robin and get out of here."

We walked through the woods, hunting, more than casually looking. Jonathan had a knife in his hand. It took me all but a second to realize it was the jeweled one I saw yesterday.

The next hit of color I spotted didn't bring any relief. Near the ground there was a rich blue color peeking past a tree. I moved around the base as my stomach dropped. Jonathan's footsteps came up behind me, as I stared frozen at the sight.

"Do you know him?" Jonathan asked.

I swallowed hard. The man was slumped against the tree,

dressed in a blue cape that stretched out beside the blood-soaked figure. The dried colors made an ugly purple hole in his chest. His eyes were open, seeing nothing anymore. A sword sat useless at his side.

My hand reached out to rest on top of his. No warmth. No coolness. Just a now dead thing.

"What was his name?" Jonathan softly prompted.

"What does it matter without the stories attached?"

"Mal..."

My hand reached up. Hovering over his face, waiting for my hand to steady before it ran over his eyelids closing them for good. I had thought this had been Robin. The added guilt of being glad it wasn't, mixed poorly with grief over the first old friend I found being already dead. "His name was Eric."

"I see you found my kill," a voice said.

Jonathan turned, slower than me as my rage demanded I rip whoever spoke apart. The man before us wore netted camouflage with bits of woven vine. A crossbow was attached to his side.

He raised his weapon at Jonathan. The tip of the crossbow's bolt glowed as if it were held in a fire. "Hunting humans is so much more fun. A deer does not worry about his past actions. There's no guilt."

"Stop talking." My words were taken as an order. The wolf at my side charged at the Huntsman. Teeth sinking around his ankle in a flash.

The man groaned in pain, but his gear kept him safer than I would have hoped. With a swift kick, Polaris backed off with a whine. Before he could aim and fire a bolt, I put myself between them.

The weapon's tip burned white hot. Drawing our

attention to magic I didn't understand.

The Huntsmen hummed happily to himself. "Delicious. Your pain and guilt would truly be a meal to feed from. I can smell the failure on you."

"Who even are you?" Jonathan asked.

When the man made no sign of answering, I volunteered. "This man was the Queen's Huntsman. His pension of eating hearts has been undersold however."

"As if an animal could judge."

Jonathan jumped at him as he spoke.

The Huntsman turned. Towering over like an angry bear on his back legs. Accepting any damage in order to grab Jonathan by the shirt. The borrowed knife went deeper, but the Huntsman didn't care all that much as he tossed Jonathan against a nearby tree.

I wanted to help. Wanted to run. To rush to Jonathan's side. To attack. So much at once. Instead, I made myself watch trying to understand what I was seeing.

"Run." My familiar refused. So loyal it made my chest ache. I could gauge how close the Huntsman was based on the wolf's growls.

"Please." I took his furry face into my hands. Pulling him close enough to lean my head against him. "He wants magical things. Go."

I was proven correct when he advanced on me, instead of Jonathan who was a vulnerable heap on the ground, still attempting to get the wind back in him.

The shadows around me shifted and whipped out at the Huntsman as he reached for me. All my memories screamed that he couldn't be here. "What are you?"

"Just another mage looking for a source of power." This

time he let the shadows engulf his hands. They left marks, but he didn't seem to notice. The Huntsman wrapped his fingers around something that should have been as intangible as smoke. And pulled.

I stumbled forward as if connected to it. Throat suddenly tight. I realized too late how literal someone could be wounded without having a single mark on their skin.

"Stop it!" Jonathan yelled.

The Huntsman lifted only a finger this time and a compulsion inside me forced me roughly to my knees. He spoke, but I couldn't hear it as my blood caught fire. Swirling sigils burned into my legs. More carved their way along my hips. Each forming as if under an invisible ember that traced a delicate shape. The process sped up along my arms and my jaw unclenched as the agony stopped just below it.

"Funny how the slightest little corruption turns all that work into weakness." His finger lifted my chin up with a touch I could barely feel. "Magic must run straight down to your soul. You're an endless act of creation."

My pulse pounded against all my senses. Maybe if I had Polaris stay, he could have saved me from the avalanche of feelings crashing against each other. Knowing he was safe was the only happy thought I could hold in my head. Then a cat.

"Dead things still live," I heard myself say. My own words clicking a new idea into place. That's why the Huntsman couldn't be here. He had already been killed by Snow White and Charming.

The realization that we had fought this battle more than once, and won, made me recognize how useless it was to do again. I screamed. Yelled so loud that the pain cleared. Then stopped. Just let go of the storm inside me. The world flooded back as I felt like a shallow echo of myself within it.

Both the Huntsman and Jonathan seemed surprised. The second now had Eric's sword in his hand and was the only one looking to me for guidance.

This time the Queen of Hearts' words came to me. "Off with his head."

Jonathan swung and neatly cleaved the Huntsmen's head from his shoulders. It fell with a thump. But no blood. "Why does this forest have so many dead things?"

Either my hearing was still off, or he was also now yelling. "You picked up on that."

He took it in stride. "There's two dead bodies on the ground. I need more than that."

"Whatever had brought him back to life also was able to keep his ability to pull magic up to the surface. In the seconds afterwards, I realized maybe the Queen of Hearts' practiced threat was from dealing with a necromancer before."

A sigh of relief deflated his shoulders. "Glad it worked."

With a nod, I pulled myself up to stand again.

"Now you're telling me that there's someone that animates corpses. This stuff never happened back home." Jonathan went on, seemingly not done with the topic. "I thought you were the darkest magic could get."

"Wow."

"I didn't mean…"

Whatever he meant or didn't mean, I waved off the rest of it. It didn't matter. My wants remained roughly the same. Find Robin. Find my dog. I looked over my arms, any bit of visible skin I could find. Rubbed at the symbols. Half expecting them to smudge and wipe away. But they stayed put. Inked into my skin. Maybe never to leave.

Chapter Eleven

"Something's coming."

"Great, what now?" Jonathan's annoyance was reaching levels it had been at this morning. Fair, this time. "Where's it coming from?"

"Everywhere." I could feel something magical nearing like an ant crawling on my skin.

By time Jonathan pulled the sword again, Polaris broke through the tree line and raced over to us. His speed made me lose footing, but I tightly held onto all fluff and muscle of the canine. "Who's my good boy?" I asked, as I ruffled up his ears.

Before Jonathan had the chance to ask why I said everywhere people appeared. A single green and several more blues grew in number until there were quite a few merry men around us.

I kissed Polaris on the snout. "You found Robin for me?"

He half sneezed; half agreed.

Robin got off his horse faster than I'd ever seen before. His haste came to a stop next to my familiar. "I thought the animal was you for a moment. Wolves are intelligent, but this one was definitely trying to communicate something more."

"He's a friend I made along the way." I wanted to grab Robin. Touch him to really prove to myself that he was there. But again, only friends. "This is Jonathan. He's been helping me find my way back."

Robin bowed his head. "Thank you."

"What are you all even doing in these woods?"

"Eric was checking into a rumor of someone Red was working with. When he hadn't returned, we formed a rescue party."

Jonathan looked down. The first sign to Robin, and soon everyone else, that something was wrong. There was a mumble of whispers, none being brave enough to ask.

"He was killed. Heart eaten for whatever magic lived within it."

Robin's face skewed. "How?"

"Was Eric investigating a necromancer? Because what it raised killed him in the end."

A cuss followed. I watched as Robin fought the same mix of grief and relief that I felt.

What I hadn't expected was for him to reach out and take my hand. "It all led us back here to find you. Fate is cruel but giving."

I smiled. No one ever could compare to him for long. "Have you returned a romantic?"

He laughed. A contagious thing that could make others feel joy even if they hadn't even heard the joke. "Well, I wouldn't go that far."

Robin's hand slipped from mine, and I fought myself to reach for it again. Not here. Not in front of everyone. If I ever could.

"It might not be a good time, but we need to gather our people." He started his speech towards us, but now was addressing the whole group. "Along with Charming's men we might be able to still stop Red Riding Hood."

"And release the Queen," Jonathan added.

Dare or not. Robin took it as one. He slowly turned to size my travel companion up. I would have given anything to know what he thought. If he approved. If he was jealous. If he hated my new friend.

"About that. Now that Malcolm is back, we know Red was lying about an exchange. We might be able to use that to our advantage."

They say the trees in Sherwood are immortal. Some believe that it is our protection that had saved them from death, disease, and drought over the years. The reverse is truer.

The tricky thing about finding this place is that it's similar to finding Neverland. You need to know which star to align yourself to, and be either guided to it, or been there before.

There was a small post built high up in a tree. A round platform nested within the branches growing through the center of it. The lookout leaned on the railing as he watched us ride by. A smile growing as he saw me. I waved.

One outpost turned into two, and the two turned into a dozen that littered the tall canopy. They varied in scope, from standing room only to nearly the size of a house. Many built in levels.

On the ground was a small path that led to the stables hidden by moss and leaf. We stopped at the mouth of the path and got off our horses as a group of men gathered. People asked how I was, where I had been, others just hugged me and said they were happy to see me back. I was so overwhelmed with the attention that I sort-of just stayed quiet and returned hugs when they came my way.

"Give him some air," Robin said. "We have much to discuss and I'm sure he can answer you all soon."

We were brought to a long winding ramp that led up to the tree houses. Familiar accessible. The floors were laid out in tiers. The first level was the largest, above was a smaller meeting room, and higher still on top was my bedroom.

"If you are going to stay, I can find you a room," Robin continued.

It took a moment for Jonathan to realize he was talking to him. He tensed, then puffed out his chest. "No more than a night or two. I must return to my sister soon."

"We can guide you out when we go meet up with Charming. Red has been advancing. Claiming the Queen's things in her absence."

"I tried to fight her on my own," I said, feeling like a failure once again. "It didn't go well. I lost my memories and that's why it took me so long to get back."

Robin's eyes flared wide. He hadn't known that me not being able to remember was even an option. "I thought you had been kidnapped and managed to get free from her. Showing up with strangers was odd enough, but you do so covered in marks I've never seen before."

If he went on, I was going to die of embarrassment.

"We need to talk," Robin decreed a bit louder for everyone. "Alone."

That word was just for me. I nodded in agreement and followed as he stepped away from the others. He climbed up, and up, until we reached my room.

"I thought you'd prefer somewhere that was yours."

My bedroom was an odd bit of extra space. There wasn't a door, more of a hatch that led to the ladder below. The roof vaulted to a point. A window without glass allowed for air to come in and the candle smoke out. There was a small seat in front of it, and my bed along a side wall.

And having Robin alone here was the stuff of my daydreams. But this situation was profoundly lacking.

"What happened to you?"

His voice held a pity I couldn't manage, and I couldn't find words to give an answer. Robin took this as an offer to investigate himself. Starting with my hands and working his way up towards my shoulders.

"This one," he said, warm hand over my upper arm. "I know this. It's the symbol on the bow you made me. Did you burn them into your skin?"

"No." The sound came too fast, and I took a second to compose myself. "The Huntsman said he wanted to feed, maybe survive off my magic. And did this to me."

"Are they everywhere?"

I nodded. He gave me a look asking for permission that made my heart stop. Context was everything. *He didn't mean it like that, Mal.*

It started with me holding out my arms for his inspection. Then his fingers pulled at my collar carefully seeing what he could as I stared at his mouth.

Robin lifted my shirt, lightly pressing on my stomach. Cold to the touch now and making me shiver. "Do they hurt?"

"No."

He chuckled. "Since when are you of so few words?"

I looked at Robin. Nothing in this room felt as much like home as he did. This rebellious boy I've known from when I was a kid. "Since when do you stick your hand up my shirt?"

"Fair enough." His eyes found mine again. "I can't begin to explain how much I missed you. You really forgot about me?" He chewed on his lip for a second before it escaped from under his teeth.

"I... I forgot myself."

He nodded a little but was glancing down and away now.

"Look at me."

For someone so often giving orders, he took them quite well. The intensity in which he did made me smile.

"Before I even had gotten my memories back, I was shown a vision of you."

"Me?"

"Yeah, you were making threats on my behalf."

He laughed nervously. Hand running over his face as he started to pace. "Maybe not my finest moment."

"I don't know about that; it was pretty flattering."

In the moonlight it looked like he blushed. Or at least I was able to convince myself that he was.

"Speaking of the exchange," he said, clearing his throat.

"I need to go plan and send a message for the meet."

"I'll help."

"No," Robin said, tone softening afterwards. "You look so tired. Stay here. The whole deal was to exchange the Queen of Hearts for your safe return. Use this time to rest."

He took a step towards the ladder below. Then paused. "I'll have people try to figure out a way to get your new familiar up here."

The image of a bunch of merry men becoming not-so-merry as they tried to lift a wolf straight up into an attic space amused me. But his way was definitely better. "Thank you."

"Of course."

Chapter Twelve

Everyone was dressed in green today. It was such a rare occurrence that even I thought I was seeing Robin multiple times. This only happened when every person was actively willing to be a killed if misidentified as him.

Jonathan and I were given clean plainclothes, and told to hang further back, which made me feel a bit homesick. I knew this would help us blend as random bystanders, but still felt wrong.

Ava agreed to meet with Robin in a grass clearing. I realized it wasn't the same one as our battle, but I couldn't fully get that place out of my head.

The Queen of Hearts was brought forward. Shoved a little towards the middle, closer to Red's Riders. The horses tense, unable to settle with the demands of those riding. They were organized, but anxious, verging on fanatic.

For the Queen's part, she hardly looked like anything. If I hadn't seen her before I would have guessed that Robin had picked a random woman off the street and made her wear a dirty ballgown found discarded somewhere. Her hair was nowhere close to the sculptured look she preferred and any makeup she once applied had faded away. Stunning how average rulers were without their trappings of power.

"We kept our end of the deal," Little John called, sound carrying as if powered by all of us. He took a few steps forward as if he was the leader.

Ava also walked closer, so she didn't have to raise her voice. Still a short distance away from the Queen, she stopped. "You're a bit too tall. My deal was with Robin."

He stepped forward. Pulling his hood down so his face could be clearly seen. "Give us Malcolm Wolf."

This seemed to please her. She grinned and started to casually pace along her side. "Let's see," she said raising a hand to her chin. "The Big Bad Wolf. Surely not a match for all these hooves." She turned towards the admiration of her Riders. They hooped and hollered.

"*Now*, Ava," Robin demanded.

She swayed back, less amused by the name. "In truth, I haven't seen that little communist apostate since he turned me into stone."

Robin took a second, making a show of his own to pretend this was news to him. "Resign then."

She laughed. The sound echoed within the chorus behind her. "The Queen's castles are quite special. Truly no place like them. I think I'll make them mine."

"Sycophant!" The true Queen spat. "I trusted you."

"My dear Queen," Red said, putting a hand to her heart as if the word wounded her. "What would I ever have done without your support?"

"I should have left you on that poster," the Queen of Hearts sneered.

Robin was already moving to put himself between the two, slowly to not set off Red's rabid following. But she was faster.

A flash of silver glimmered under the sun for a second before it was sunk into the Queen's stomach. "It seems no one has use for you anymore."

Red stepped back quickly, and Robin moved in to put pressure on the Queen's wound. Hands soon covered in blood. The whole time the Queen just stared wordlessly up at someone she hadn't cared about when she had the power to do anything.

"Take your men home now, and I won't be forced to burn every forest in this kingdom, so you truly have no place to return home to." Ava wiped the blade on her sleeve, the blood matching the existing red.

Chapter Thirteen

"I fucked up bad, Mal." Robin said, to an otherwise empty conference room that sat high above most of the other tree houses. Always lit, day or night. A beacon that there was always a meeting place for everyone. Whenever they needed, with whoever they needed.

He had already given an impassioned speech to the others about how it didn't really matter if the Queen of Hearts was dead or not. That she had been a dictator, and her death could even be celebrated by those she had harmed. How not a one of us hadn't been touched in some way by her oppressive systems.

But here, just the two of us, his regrets were clear. "That bad-bad, huh?" I teased. Like I always did when something hit the level of stressing him out enough that he said both bad and Mal in the same sentence. He was the only one who ever could without blaming me.

"I'm not joking." His chaotic pacing winded down as he took a seat.

"I know you aren't."

"What do we do now?"

"Your plan still works. We let Charming know that we were unable to get, well, either of them to resign. As expected. And we fight another day. Maybe we still use me as a surprise. Maybe we don't."

He nodded along, as if being told the plan for the first time instead of just being reconvinced that his own idea had merit. Robin took a breath and rested a tired head on his hand. "How do you do that?"

"Do what?"

"Make me believe in things again."

"Oh, don't ask me." I laughed and finished off the drink I had been nursing the whole meeting. This group had never followed me. Despite what Rapunzel's chess board claimed. Robin is the one who kept the wheels on the operation. I was the radical one known for picking fights and saying things out of turn. "Remember when we would sneak out? We never went far. Just enough where we could lie on the grass and forget that the world was bigger than the two of us."

He smiled. The first time all day. "Do familiars need walks like other animals?"

That was the mischief. The one thing of Robin that always got saved for me. "They must."

Robin figured out that he could even get my not-so-wild wolf friend to play fetch with him. To be honest, I'm not sure who was enjoying it more. Me watching. Robin playing. Or the magically bonded animal.

I was lying down, keeping an eye on them as Robin sat up with a growing laziness to his throws. After one of the throws Polaris decided not to give Robin the stick. He leaned in on his paws and just chewed on it.

"I've never seen anything like him," Robin declared.

If I could have shrugged, I would have. The attempt ended up more of a stretch. "The Beast made him for me. I've heard of mages having owls and cats before but nothing so…" *Violent.* That's the word I wanted. Felt wrong to say given he just snapped the stick in half and awkwardly tried to spit the pieces out.

"And these," Robin continued. He took my hand and if this was a new habit of his I was going to die happy. His hands were smaller than mine, but not by a great deal. The difference seeming even less when he used both of his to study my one.

"I think they would help me do magic even easier now," I said, as Robin looked up at me. "Like your bow uses sigils to store magic that only activates when shooting."

He nodded even though I swear I could be saying gibberish. "When you first tried to make an enchanted weapon. The string vibrated too strong and snapped."

"Hurt like hell when it hit me."

He laughed and he released my hand. Taking a second to clear a spot from leaves before lying down next to me. "Have you done magic since this?"

I shook my head and turned to look up at the sky. Afraid, mostly.

"Try."

When I didn't answer he poked me in the side, so I'd look at him. "Maybe I need incentive." It was a poor choice of words because given how close he was I could only think

110

of one thing I wanted.

I swallowed hard, feeling my Adam's apple bob in my throat. Hyperaware of too much now. The pine scent from the trees. The tension in Robin's muscles. When I managed to pull my eyes away from his lips, I realized he was looking somewhere he wasn't meant to either.

"We should try." Robin's hand reached over to touch the sigil on my neck. I leaned in making his hold a little tighter on my throat and found his mouth greeted me halfway. He parted his lips, deepening the kiss.

I actually thought of the Frog Prince for a moment. How he knew my feelings, more openly than I had been with them. How I joked about first kisses being magic. My skin tingled under Robin's touch.

The shift made him break the kiss. Robin opened his eyes and lifted his fingers just barely off my skin to see. "I knew you had it in you."

I smirked. "Leaders need to better mind their word choices." This time I was certain a blush rose to his cheeks. I could feel the heat of it myself. "Tell me what you need."

"You aren't going to like my answer."

"No?"

"Be serious."

"I'm a wild thing."

Robin pulled away in order to sit up. I sat up too, as he looked ahead of him at a patch of grass by his feet. Maybe I shouldn't have reminded him of responsibility. Maybe the kiss was just to elicit strong emotions in me. My fear of not being able to do magic dissolved into multiple new worries. Would we ever be more than what we were now?

But, I knew this look at least. It said 'I'm sorry. I can't play right now, Mal. Please help me with something else.'

"Just tell me the plan."

Chapter Fourteen

Least I got to look epic for this annoying stealth first operation. Dressed in a hooded black cloak and gambeson armor underneath. Face covered from the bridge of my nose down. The wolf walking at my side didn't make me look inconspicuous. Rather someone not to mess with on an official quest from somewhere. The covertness came from the fact that I didn't look like my normal self. Not a merry man, nor in a tailored coat over hand-me-down extras from a port worker too far from the sea.

The official story was to escort two siblings from Rapunzel's tower to meet with Snow White. Jonathan was too old to be a playmate, but Sophie was the age of their son.

All of this to keep Robin's alliance with Prince Charming more of a secret and deliver news of the Queen's death. If Red didn't know I had returned, nor that we had a royal army waiting in the wings to join our resistance fighters we'd have a chance at stopping her from taking control of the rest of the Queen's men.

It was clear that the Cards hadn't been given new orders yet. Some defected upon the spell on them being broken, most however, continued to serve the princes and princesses they had been in her absence. They cleared out of the way as we crossed a stone bridge and walked through open gates to a delegation of Cirrus' tutors. He had grown a foot since I last saw him. All proper form and manners except for the bored expression on his face.

Sophie stepped forward, standing between the two groups, and curtsied in front of Cirrus. She'd had been so worried she would mess the gesture up that along the way she practiced with every bird, bunny, and us endlessly. All the cramming did make her look quite the proper young lady. "It's nice to meet you Cirrus White."

"As it is you, Lady Conall," he replied with a bow of his own. "We are scheduled to play in the garden at noon." However, the sigh that followed was quite unapproved.

"Young sir," I said, and pulled down my mask. His eyes widened upon recognizing me. "The lady is quite tired from her travels. Maybe we could move inside away from the sun."

"Certainly. We can join my father in his reading room."

His tutors all too used to this ploy, and always eager for an excuse to get their charge near books brought us into the house. Calling a two-story library, a reading room was selling it a bit short. The walls were painted with ivy that seamlessly bled into wood carved bookshelves with a ceiling decorated with the clouds Cirrus was named after.

"Wow," Sophie breathed out. She walked further into the room ignoring any proper guidance we'd given her. "It would take a lifetime to finish every book in here. Do people buy books they don't need?"

Jonathan shrugged. Either not knowing the answer, or not wanting to explain that people indeed did buy things for the sheer fun of it.

A man dressed in white with gold pauldrons sat up in his seat. "Cirrus, what's going on?"

His son took a spot next to him. Collapsing into an armchair with no pretense. "Your playmates showed instead."

"Hello Charming," I grinned as I moved closer.

"Mal?" He stood, not looking convinced it was me. My company didn't help place me either. His eyes narrowed, then jaw dropped in surprise. A second later, he threw his arms wide and gave me a hug. "You're alright. I thought—Never mind what I thought. I'm glad you're okay."

Charming pulled back, still grinning. "That means you two are actually sent by Robin?"

"Name's Jonathan," he said holding out his hand to shake. "We have some unfortunate news."

He blew a sigh out, preparing for whatever, as he gestured for Jonathan to take a seat. "Thank you for bringing some good news along with you."

I winked at him. An earnest compliment even from a married man still made me feel things.

"Cirrus, why don't you show your guest around?"

He looked ready to complain, but Sophie's earnest staring at all the books, changed his expression. "Okay, Dad." Cirrus walked over to her with a new curiosity. "You can touch them. Books are meant to be read."

"I know but…" Sophie nervously laughed. "They are so pretty."

"Come on." Cirrus leaned in the direction of a shelf. "I can show you my closest friends."

"Cassandra is dead?!" Charming raised his voice with

alarm. He waved the tutors away, before he thought better of it, hand now telling them to stop. "Please bring Snow here."

I was equally relieved as I was concerned that I had missed Jonathan starting in on everything he was told to report about. "If Red is back, and there's no Queen, a coup will follow. One that will have nothing in its way. Unless we do something." I said, and hoped I wasn't repeating something he just heard.

"It's time," Charming said. He leaned back in his chair, shaking his head.

"Why is there a wild animal in our house?" Snow asked, giving it a wide birth. Polaris lifted his head but put it down once pets weren't coming. "Malcolm?"

I didn't even manage to get my hello out before my second hug of the day came. "Missed you both."

She hummed a noise that I had long ago learned meant 'visit more, silly'. Snow walked around to the back of her husband's chair, putting a hand on his shoulder. "What's happened?"

"War is coming."

Pretending we were just a visiting family enjoying the White's beach like an extended shared vacation was wearing on me. Or maybe I was just feeling hot under all the black while the royal family and guests stripped down to swimwear.

When Charming was a lost boy, he had two scars on each side of his chest. Now he sat out here perfectly content with

116

his body, wife, and son playing. Sure, war wasn't great. But even still, he looked happier than ever.

Cards stood a respectful distance away. Their tasks mingled with the standing force the family trained and controlled. I watched them go about as if no Queen was simply fine. Near mindlessly just following the next authority in line. "Will the Queen's remaining men join you?"

Snow looked over watching them with me now. Twirling a parasol idly in her hands. "I wouldn't bet our lives on it. As soon as a new ruler is appointed, any order we give can be superseded."

"We are running out of time then," Jonathan started. The sounds of Sophie and Cirrus splashing around made for a strange background to his words. "Robin will have to make his move before the Riders do."

Charming ran a hand along his chin stubble, strategizing as he watched his son play. "One of my scouts returned a few days ago. Red has set up a base in the Queen's summer castle. Return to Sherwood. My men can meet you at the manor. We will stop her there."

"If this works," Snow continued. "We will need to use the Treaty of the Nine to install a new leader. If Red cares about the law at all, we can use it against her."

Chapter Fifteen

I returned alone the next afternoon. And by evening the men had gone full ritualistic on the eve of a battle. They always celebrated beforehand. Using it as an excuse to touch, be touched, and eat their fill without fear of having to ration things. It was an excuse to do anything you had been holding out to do. Except drinking. That was saved for victory.

It barely counted as making rounds given the distance, as I walked around the extended rope bridges that linked all the tree houses together. Finding candles burning low and cups of paint sat out everywhere. Checking both occasionally to make sure they'd last the rest of the night.

Finally, I settled in what was normally a dining room. Polaris apparently decided to party in his own way and was sitting on top of the table tilting his head as two men painted thick bands of color on each other's faces.

He was a smart animal, but I didn't think our understanding of each other could go far enough to explain that this was all about leaving a mark on someone. If a friend were to fall, you'd have their colors with you still through the end of the battle.

Movement by the door caught my eye, and I smiled as Robin walked in. Arms covered with handprints, and a cup of paint in his own hand. "It's a sin that you think you can sit in here untouched."

I leaned back on the table, raising a brow. "You planning to do something about it?"

He nodded, and I hungrily watched him as he set the paint on the table. Green. *His color.* "Ready?"

The other people in the room came our way then moved past to celebrate elsewhere paying no mind to us. I watched them silently until we were alone.

Robin dipped his finger into the paint, and I closed my eyes so he could more easily place a dark band of green across my face. His fingers moved a piece of my hair out of the way as he made sure the color ran across the whole way. "I'm sorry about before."

"What you mean?" I peeked an eye open to check if he was done. Then the other when he was staring down not really looking at anything.

He chewed on his bottom lip, hard enough that I wanted to tell him to be nicer to something so soft and lovely.

"The first time you vanished I thought I lost my chance. Left alone missing my best friend. Everything that could be. But we didn't really have control in that." He looked up at me. "But this time... I sent you away. If you didn't come back, it would have been on me."

"It's fine." I pushed off the table and moved over to snag the mirror the others had left to check Robin's handywork. "It was only to Snow's castle."

After traveling the length of the table and back, Robin

was still standing there looking upset. "Is this really bothering you? There wasn't any trouble in the slightest."

"Thankfully." Robin's jaw was clenched tight enough I was surprised he managed to even get that sound out.

"It's a mistake I refused to make again," he blurted all at once. "We should actually try this."

Shock made me doubt my ears. "Try what?"

"I—I don't want it to sound like an order. But your place is with me. Was before this battle. Will be after it."

"Please stop talking."

"Sorr—"

I put my hand over his mouth, pushing him back away from the door, and out of sight from party goers down the hall. Holding us still until they passed by proved easy. Robin being so cooperative, eyes locked on me, waiting for a next command. The look made my stomach flip.

"I've waited my whole life to hear you say that." I pulled my hand away, wanting to taste him. Mess up the still drying paint on my face, get it all over him. "Not here though. We'll get caught."

"My room's closer."

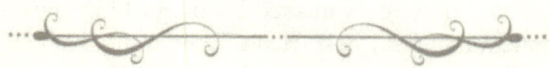

We flipped the lock the second we made it to his room. Refusing to waste another moment more of our lives.

I kissed Robin as if he were the only good thing in this world. When his tongue brushed over my lip, I felt magic flare. Fuzzy like an excitable drink. Take that negative triggers, I could glimmer too.

Robin took half a step back, dazed. And my enjoyment was suddenly teetering on if this was akin to a drunken mistake. His hand rose to his mouth, licking slowly and making the skin glisten as if savoring my touch. "Did you know your magic has a taste to it?"

"Yeah." I reached for him. Fingers catching under the edge of his shirt hem and pulling him back. "Is it weird?"

"It's like blackberries. Or something tart."

Not what I meant, but I took it as a compliment.

"I need more." His mouth pressed against mine while I was still grinning before falling into place comfortably locked between.

His hands found their way under my own shirt. Touching me with as much desperate want that I thought only I carried this whole time. A moan vibrated through me in tune with the magic and Robin breathed it all in deeply like the air itself. A little magical piece of me now within him.

I couldn't take just standing here only kissing anymore. I pushed him forward taking control of our movements and guiding us to the bed like a dance.

Robin fell with a playful push onto his hodgepodge of blankets. I had planned to instantly move on top, but damn, this sight was worthy of an extra second too.

"Would you come here?" Robin laughed.

"Yes sir." I grinned. We kissed slower this time, with all the passion and pent-up desire years had built. His hips rolled, grinding into me.

My mouth moved to his jaw, then ear, before dragging teeth down his neck, stopping to suck on his pulse point. Definitely worth it as Robin made a pleased noise without a single thing to muffle the sound.

His hands alongside my face pulled me back to his mouth, kissing me feverishly. I could taste smoke as I took a second to catch myself.

I breathed the magic out and it hung visible in the air like a cold night. Half translucent and swirling as Robin took it with a sense of greed, I've never witnessed in him before. Dizzyingly attractive on an otherwise selfless man.

Robin moaned and rolled his head to the side against the bed. I leaned back to check on him and saw his eyes flash gold as a shiver rolled through his body.

"You aren't just in this for my magic, are you?" I teased, finding it too hot to care about the answer.

His head rolled back to look up at me. Smiling at something. "Mal, don't you get it? It's you. It's all you. Everywhere. Drowning out ev—ery..."

I grinned, wide enough to surely show fang if I had any. My hand had interrupted his words by firmly pressing against his erection. "If you keep talking like that, I'm not going to be held responsible for what I want next."

"Be irresponsible," he said, as I stroked his length a few times, just enough to leave him wanting more. "Be the most irresponsible you've ever..." Robin mouthed the last word, nose flaring as my hand dipped under the fabric of his pants.

I was fairly sure his babbling dissolved into repeating my name over and over in prayer. My hand found him hard and eager for my touch. Feeling Robin, the noble thief with a gold heart, melt in my hands made me want more. Want everything. This second. I pulled back so I could return myself the favor of feeling a part of him inside my mouth.

As I went to lean in, there was a knock on the door. We both froze despite the door being locked. I should have ignored it. Made Robin silently quake, attempt a reply without giving away what we were doing. But when Little

John's voice followed, I knew that fantasy would have to wait. "Sir, an envoy is here."

I'd happily killed that messenger if we hadn't been friends. Doubted he was even standing outside the door waiting for a reply. How long have we waited for this moment already?

"Mal," Robin said, shifting to sit up.

"Right." I moved away, adjusting myself as Robin packed the show away.

He sat up, looking me over. "We should have done this sooner. All the other moments where we had time. Instead of now, trying to prevent a civil war."

"Yeah."

He unlocked the door, hand pausing on the handle. "I'm not done with you. Not ever. Know that."

"Okay." Our timing kept being horribly poor. All the good in me was already devoted to this man. I'd follow him into a literal war. Sex or no sex. Still hearing the kind words mattered, and I felt stronger for it. "Let's go save the lands."

Polaris ran out ahead of us as we greeted Charming's envoy. Which ended up being Jonathan. He stood on the forest floor looking up at the festivities above with an expression that didn't make me want to offer an invite right away.

Having not seen me that long ago he went straight into it. "I don't know if I should be flattered or insulted how useful a commoner who can read seems to be to all these royals."

"Pick flattered," Robin said. "What message do you have?"

Jonathan pulled forward his bag and took out a rolled-up wax sealed parchment. I watched as it was handed over. Expecting merely words and was surprised to see an annotated drawing of Charming's forces.

"This is amazing, thank you," Robin said, and instantly became deeply absorbed in all the ways he could use this info. Seemed rude to me, but Jonathan actually looked complimented, so I let it be.

"Where's Sophie?" I asked.

"With Snow White and Cirrus. Felt like a line too far to bring her into a battle where we storm a castle." He shook his head. "What have I gotten myself into?"

"Besides quickly becoming everyone's favorite map maker?" He let out a nervous laugh and I decided he needed some paint too. "Come on, let me unofficially make you part of our group."

Part Three: Crowning Achievement
Chapter Sixteen

The Queen only visited a castle when it was in season, leaving our would-be battleground overgrown. The trimmings clashed with leaves that had turned yellow and orange. Where they should have been blooms, there were only dormant buds.

There were men making rounds on horseback, but the grounds weren't crawling with Cards or Riders. Hopefully, a good sign that we would be able to pull off our ambushes.

Robin moved out in front, dressed in full armor under his hood. He walked down the line of gathered merry men. Far less than what Charming would be able to hopefully provide. But good men, ones we both trusted. "The narrative they wish to tell us," he shouted, "is that nothing we do matters. Let's prove them wrong today."

Cheers were shouted as Robin moved back into formation next to me. I hadn't seen Charming, or any other friendly soldiers, but a figure in the distance was holding my attention. It sat like an extra shadow cast next to a tree.

"Ready?"

"Huh?" I looked to Robin and then back to where I had been focusing, and the silhouetted shape was gone. "Yes, of course."

Traveling with Jonathan had always made me feel like the oddball who could do magic. But here with merry men I was in like company. "Mages on my mark!"

"Now!" I brought my arms out, left crossing over right, fanning my fingers apart as if to play separate strings. The motion was mirrored by the group as the mages among us did the same.

A shield formed, each of us providing a stable piece of it for ourselves and the men around us. We marched forward, protected as arrows shot through the sky towards us. They shimmered against the protective spell, falling safely away, and becoming trampled under our boots.

Robin and the other archers returned fire. Their arrows tipped with our magic and allowed through. Those that remained waited and fought back with steel against anyone who attempted to rush us.

The skirmish grew the attention of anyone tasked with protecting the castle. Their numbers would quickly overwhelm us if we didn't break off soon. Swords drawn, teeth bared, magic flying. Jonathan was in the thick of it as Robin and I played defense at a distance.

"Split up!" Robin yelled. At his warning I closed my palms making each piece of the magical protection pop like a firecracker. One with intent, knowing exactly what it took to maim others while avoiding us. He glanced around to check for any wounded among our ranks before running ahead. "Mal, with me."

Polaris and I happily ran after him.

We had nowhere near the reach that he did with that

bow. Robin sent arrows into the hands, legs, or the chest of any soldier who was still 'just following orders' along our path to find Red. Climbing several stairs to reach a higher ring of the palace. I covered the best I could by siphoning off the magic from the mages among them.

Around a corner was a surprisingly close Card, but Polaris was already on top of him before I even registered it was a person.

Several yards away was another clash. Men on foot slashed at Riders as their horses tried to box them against a wall.

Charming's order could be heard over it. "Move inside! They can't fight well if not on horseback."

As they fled, one of the Riders pulled the reigns and directed her horse to barrel our way. Robin tracked the shot and released an arrow.

The Rider fell from their horse landing in a lump near us and the animal continued past us. I watched it run free as if it had never wanted any of this.

"She was like a scarecrow."

I looked back to a body that had dead looking eyes and far too wide of a grin on her face. "Do you get the feeling that we are being led somewhere?" I nudged the body with my boot. Not a single twitch.

Robin brought a hand to his mouth. "People don't naturally die this fast from a wound."

"Malcolm!" A voice called from a balcony above us. Jonathan was standing with a few merry men. They must have regrouped along their own path as we were watching Charming. Jonathan pointed across to another building.

Standing on the roof was a man with a top hat. Thin, almost nothing but skin and bones. A hand rose to the brim, and he tipped his head down towards us. The Cheshire cat smile, and dead bodies. Was he the necromancer? It made more sense than a cook climbing up to the roof for protection.

Another Rider from the group that broke off as Charming's men escaped came our direction. Her body glowed with magic.

I lifted my hand and pictured ripping the air from her lungs. She coughed out tuffs of magic. Her horse given mixed signals as she leaned forward to use him as support. The animal verged off in between another building. This soldier was clearly different than the one Robin shot. She was still alive.

What was left of the spell the Rider had been casting pooled in my hand with a mint like coolness. It felt like clarity. "We are courting injury by fighting blindly. I want to try something. Can you cover me?"

"Depends on where you are going."

"Physically? Nowhere." I meditated, letting the magic pick up on my intent as it rolled through me. Smoke splashed upon the floor like a waterfall. Then spread out in a liquid pool flowing away. All my senses unifying with it to see the path of least resistance.

Sunshine sparkled on dew heavy leaves. Bursts of color from pink roses, and yellow lilies. The bleeding body of one of Charming's men was soaking up excess water from rain we had missed. In the middle of the vision, Red herself. She corrected the hood that had slipped in battle.

"I know where to find her." I looked up at Jonathan signaling him and the others forward to follow.

The greenhouse made it easy to know we found the right building because of its wood framed glass walls. It was a large enough area that Red's details were muddled into nothing at from this distance. Black uniformed mages stood guard making sure Red had her fun without getting overwhelmed.

Their movements snapped out of attention as we neared. Waiting for us to get within range or to fall back if Red decided to move from the building behind them.

Polaris howled at my feet as smoke began to billow in the tight space between buildings. Rising up in a suffocating cloud within seconds.

The air buzzed with magic. I grinned and joined Polaris's howl with a taunt. "Who's afraid of the Big Bad Wolf?"

One of the Riders turned her back to the oncoming fight. Banging her hand against the glass to their leader. "Help us!" Red must have done an exceptionally good job of painting me as a villain. The pleading knocks lifted Red's head as she watched.

A few weapons clattered against the ground in the moment of silence that fear created just before. The figure in the distance started to slowly move away.

"Attack!" Another Rider screamed trying to rally the few that were left. They threw their own magic and it caught flame against ours, blowing back like a burning wind.

Charming ran into the scene, sliding to a stop at the mouth of the alleyway. Pebbles kicked up as the smoke cleared. "Not to break up the quick work, but did you guys bring another ally?"

"Uh?" Robin started. "Just you."

"My men keep spotting people draped in black veils. Faces covered as they throw magic about. They seem to be on our side. One was attacked by us, and it crumbled into a pile of dust as if to just avoid the blow instead."

"It has to be that necromancer that tried to kill Jonathan

and me."

Charming mumbled his concern. "Clearly not on our team after all."

"I wouldn't be sure they are on anyone's side at this point. If they want to help us today, fine. We need to finish what we started first."

"She's gone." Robin gestured. "Now where?"

Charming glanced over, taking a moment to think. "The other entrance connects to the throne room."

We ran through the greenhouse and out, trying to catch up as fast as possible. The plants swayed with the breeze of us all running past.

"You." Red hissed as we reached the inner keep's doors. "Wishing for war, or is this just because I put blood on your name?"

Prince Charming pushed past me. "By order of the Treaty of Nine. Step away from the throne."

Red turned as if she hadn't seen it literally an inch from her. "This throne?" she asked, before making a deliberate show to sit down. Even adjusting her cloak as if we would be painting the scene. "Laws come into existence as easy as they can leave it. Especially ones written to protect whosoever sits right here."

An arrow flew and bit into her shoulder. Her hand made quick work to baby the injury. The indignity of it seemed to cause an equal amount of pain as she gritted her teeth. "Do you have nothing to give but violence?"

"Not to authority," Robin said.

"War will tell." She ripped the arrow out, and the wound glowed. "I'm the Queen now!" Her face was almost the color of her nomenclature. "Leader of the Riders. Head of the House of Cards. Ruler of the Nine Lands."

Her magic got brighter. A shadow on the floor spread out as if spilled over the smooth floor. Robin glanced over to me before moving back like everyone else.

"This isn't me."

A shape rose up to form a figured covered in black, details coming into focus last. Hat included. Tuffs of hair escaped from under it with big brown eyes full of contempt as he glanced over to Red. "Tell me, why would an anarchist care about your titles?"

"I order you to defend me!"

The man took his hat into his boney hands, with a soberness that seemed slow compared to her fury. "You've overstepped your reach."

"My reach is whatever I can take," she spat back. "Whatever happened to your other body?"

"The one that made me look more like you?" The Hatter tilted his head away. "Didn't like it anymore."

"You used me," Red sneered, not seeming to care that she was about to face a battle on multiple fronts.

The Hatter snorted. "Let's just say," he said, taking a few steps to stand alongside Robin and me. "I'm feeling a bit merrier than before."

I stepped forward, wolf at my heels. But was forced to stop as the Hatter blocked my way with an arm. My eyes rose to meet his.

His face was young but looked as if he'd seen far too much for me to correctly guess his real age. "Death is easy. Living is hard." He set the hat back on his head before continuing. "Every monied cat and hired pig would have us eating cake all day."

Robin not feeling the need to figure out what this Mad Hatter was saying charged forward. Yelling for everyone with us to fight.

Charming's men, Jonathan, and every other person on our side jumped into the fray.

"The House is still at my command," Red yelled. Her magic pulled back to unveil a wall of Cards that would need to be fought first.

As weapons clashed, I started to smell fire. I backed off to find where it was coming from. The flames licking at drapes caught my attention. Scuffling soldiers moved, and I saw they'd knocked over a candle. Once lit, the blaze moved fast up the curtains.

They vanished from their rod moments later, only to be whipped towards Robin by Red like a burning extension of her cape. "You are nothing. What do you even have in this world? A bunch of trees?"

There was a growl. A Card swung a dagger at me. I barely avoided it thanks to the heads up from Polaris. Spinning around, I put the attacker in a choke hold.

Pain ran through my core, and I shoved the Card away to check myself for injury. Nothing. My head seemed to whisper a name. And I looked for Robin.

He'd been knocked to the ground. Defiant looking with the bold paint across his face.

"You will die before I know your real name," Red taunted. She spun her arms around to cast a hell of a spell that made the whole room brighter.

It cast a large shadow behind Robin. As the spell crashed down, I willed myself to where I desired. Now standing between them with my arms raised out over to protect Robin.

Her spell pushed and curled around to show a ghostly sword that had been summoned against my palms.

"The brighter the light," Robin laughed, still on his knees under my protection. "The better the shadow."

I tilted the sword and drove it into the ground. A shockwave of magic lashed out. Engulfing any light. "Maybe death is too good for you."

With a spark, a circle was etched around us on the ground. Shining harshly and blocking everything outside of it from sight as arcane symbols finished the design.

"I know your true form." My smile grew wider. "Elle avoit vû le loup." The words made the engravement shine with blinding illumination.

Robin was right. Everything tasted tart like blackberries. My mouth grew dry from watering. The battle around us sounded like off key notes being played.

Chapter Seventeen

A pig stood in front of me. A third of my height, and unable to meet my eye. I stared at the farm animal still too out of my head to figure out how it got here. My attention had to refocus at a close distance as hands cupped my face. Their impossible coolness brought my focus swimming back.

"Are you okay?" Robin asked. "Do you remember who you are? Know who I am?"

Who cared who I was? I'd kill to be this man's clothes. Tightly cling to his magnificent form.

"Please Mal, I'm begging you. Not again."

Malcolm. That was my name. I shook my head as the pieces fell into place. "Sorry. Transmutation makes my head... bubbly."

He gave me a 'no shit' sort of expression. One hand refused to leave my cheek even as he turned saying something to the others with us. *Wait*, no. I had put my hand over his and hadn't let him go.

"Catch the animal," Charming yelled. His guards did as

he said. The remaining Cards glanced around at the scene before them trying to figure out if they were also meant to follow him, or a literal pig now.

Our men didn't hesitate as they started binding together the hands of anyone who hadn't fled. I looked over the sweat drenched faces and realized it would be a different game from here on out. What was left of Red's hood was smoldering on the ground. Someone gave it an extra stomp to put it out the rest of the way.

Robin and I headed outside paying no attention to any horrors that may lay around us. I didn't understand what my role in this new world would be. Wasn't the throne. Succession would be a matter of voting royals. It wasn't healing the wounded either.

The necromancer however, seemed able to fill in that role. With a whirl of his fingers, firefly-like glow appeared, landing on what bled and pulled the seams of the person back together.

His magic felt as foreign as mine must have to Jonathan. "Could you teach me that trick?" I called over to him.

The Hatter looked up and smiled. "Do you know how opals form?"

"Is that the answer?"

He laughed. "Not quite."

The Hatter moved from what he was doing and away from us. The small lights floated off to another person.

"Hey wait!" I quickly moved to catch up to him. "You keep showing up. Can I have a name?"

"This bodies, or mine?"

"Ah," Robin said, at my side. "That's why Red both knew you. And didn't."

He nodded. "The last body was called Lillie. That form is back in the ground now."

Robin smiled softly. "Might be a better world if we could all change as we desired."

"I like you," The Hatter declared. "My name is Madison."

"Alright, Madison," I said, name rolling around in my mouth. "Do you know what's next?"

"Same as always. Death and power struggles."

"Bit cynical from someone who seems to..." I waved a hand at his current form. "Defy both."

He waved back, gesturing to Robin and me. "This is cute. I like it."

"Thank you?" Robin said, looking over to me.

The news came like a tidal wave. We had left a void in our wake and now no one knew who should fill that spot on high. Any name was instantly fought against. "Actually, if Ariel wanted to rule, she should have visited the land more often. You can't trust a royal like that."

I stopped even paying attention to who was saying what. Just endless debates that made no progress. I ignored it all the best I could since it would come down to a vote anyways.

Snow was leading the forum, but even she was barely overseeing things since most of the royals still had to travel to reach her land. We expected the third and possibly fourth of the nine to show today.

Letters were delivered to me by evening. The first of which contained a deed to a piece of land. I read over everything trying to figure out the why and where of it, until Ava's name stood out. She had no heir, so what was hers was now mine. I ripped the other envelopes open.

One had a key that must belong to some treasurer somewhere. The last of the bunch was about Red Riding Hood herself, rather than her estate. I must have made a mess as Snow circled around.

"What did you get?" she asked.

"It's a letter from the White Knight," I said, distractedly trying to figure out when I last saw her.

"Oh, how is she?"

"She's found a pig…"

I asked Robin to accompany me, but despite my best attempts he insisted that he had to stay and make sure no royal conscripted any merry man into their guard as replacements. But encouraged me to finish what I thought had to be done.

My thoughts bitterly spat up the memory of Robin saying my place was with him, that he wouldn't make the mistake of letting me go again at nauseum until the happy memory started to be tinted, and I forced myself to think about who else I could get to go with me.

The royals were out, and anyone with any sort of official duty would be busy. I headed outside and found Cirrus, Jonathan and Sophie playing a ball game on the beach.

"Do you by chance remember when the Queen purged

all the knights?"

Jonathan glanced over. He rushed forward to hit the ball back to the younger kids before feeling secure enough to answer me. "Vaguely. Why?"

"Would you like to go visit one?"

Cirrus and Sophie scored on him when he wasn't looking. He scoffed then shook his head and left the court. "One more adventure together?"

"Once more." I smiled. "Camping like the good ol' days."

We rode to the site mentioned in the letter, the area feeling truly wild and free. The land was lush. Full of weeds that would normally get trampled to make the paths clear for foot traffic.

The wind rustled chimes, each carefully strung together with wood and glass beads. The only other human touch to the area was a small hut built from the plants around us sitting between it all.

A woman ducked her head out to greet us. "Take Red from the Riders and what remains?" she said, as she stood to her full height. Faded armor creaked with the movement.

Subtraction. That's the answer she wanted. Old riddles from when we'd been much merrier men. "I didn't know this is where you'd been since you left."

"Now you do." Her head turned away from me. "Who might you be?"

"Jonathan." His wide eyes stared up at her. "My father

used to tell me grand stories about knights, madam."

"Those days are over," she started to move around to the side of the hut. "I was hunting bigger things until this pig here fell into a trap." We followed, seemingly all caught up in our own reasons.

A caged animal sat under several hanging bird houses. "How do you know it's her, instead of just some random pig?"

"Maybe the poets will say it's the eyes."

They didn't look any different to me. Pigs already had human-like eyes. Or at least this breed did. "Polaris, what do you think?"

The wolf ventured forward slowly. Nose going into overdrive with audible sniffs. Once he got close, he pulled back, teeth snarling.

"That's a well-trained wolf," the White Knight said.

Jonathan was still looking at her as if she were made of the bright beautiful moon. "I'm sure you could train one similarly."

She crossed her muscular arms over her chest and looked him over again. If he made her angry, she could snap him in two. "You always have the queerest friends, Mal."

I tilted my head at the two of them. "Considering keeping him?"

"Nah, we have business." She winked at Jonathan before gesturing to the cage. "If I let her go, she will just eat all the food I put out. Greedy little thing. Smart enough to avoid most traps with ease, until I realized what was happening."

"Kill it."

Jonathan's head jerked back. "Mal."

"I admit it isn't the usual way we'd do things." It was

silent enough that I could hear the chimes in the front again. "But maybe sometimes we should. Has this cycle not gone on long enough?"

"You sure?" the White Knight asked.

I reached into my jacket and pulled out the deeds and pushed them into her chest. "Eat the rich."

She caught the papers so they wouldn't fall as I turned and walked away. "Where are you going?"

"There's an empty throne, and I'm determined to make sure someone decent sits in it."

"Guess we'll be going, madam." Jonathan said nervously, as he lagged behind.

She laughed softly. "It's Marsha."

I swung up on my horse and waved a goodbye. "Enjoy your dinner."

Chapter Eighteen

The hall wasn't decorated to the nines. Soft curtains billowed in from the open windows. Coming just short of reaching the chairs positioned around a large circular table.

I sat in the back along with several traveling aids from the various royals. Sophie and Cirrus were also among the audience that were watching the busy debate over who should rule them all.

The only person moving was the bald-headed bow tied man we'd found sitting on top of Prince Phillip's rose wall. Seemed Humphrey discovered his next job.

He took notes anytime someone spoke at the table. No matter how big or small. He looked a bit worse for wear, as if Prince Phillip had ordered him pushed off, but hadn't been able to put all the pieces back together in time.

"We need all of the nine to be here for a proper vote," a Princess of Heart that I hadn't met said. She had beautifully black hair that was tied in a long ponytail.

"Nonsense," another said. Handsome for sure, but I had even less idea of his name. "There's a majority here if we can come to an agreement ourselves."

That caused a scandal and Humphrey broke into a sweat trying to record everyone's overlapping voices. Hours in, I figured it was going to be another day of circular arguments and happily resigned myself to petting Polaris between his ears.

"There are six of us here," Snow said, trying to get the conversation on a productive track. "If five of us agree then that's what shall be done."

"Wolf."

Both me and Polaris glanced up to see Rapunzel staring our way. By the angle I think she was speaking to me, but I didn't understand why.

"You want someone without royal blood to rule?" The raven-haired Princess asked.

"Why not a promotion?" Rapunzel said. "It can happen in chess."

"Wait, what?" I suddenly wanted to sink down and hide behind my familiar. Maybe if they couldn't see me, they wouldn't think to ask me for things.

"My vote is also for Malcolm," Prince Henri said, lifting a glass to me.

"Agreed," Charming said. Snow shot him a glance, and a smile of approval.

"I think the wolves can handle it," the Beast said. Prince Phillip took a moment then lifted his drink as well.

Snow clapped her hands together, summoning everyone's attention. "Five makes a majority. Do you accept?"

"Before he speaks," Rapunzel said, suddenly pushing her chair out to stand. She walked over to me. Expression tight. "A gift."

Rapunzel took my hand, turning it over to press something into it. "You reached the 8th Rank," she said softly so only I could hear. And when she pulled back a chess piece sat in my palm. A queen.

"This was a bad idea," I said. My knee kept nervously bouncing and my hands busy adjusting a far too heavy crown that had been placed on my head. Never before had someone like me been made a king.

I had been convinced only long enough to say one tiny word. An utterance really. It took grand talks of change. How systems never before accessible to commoners would now be under my rule. At the time, Sophie had been staring up at me with a bright excited expression nodding an encouragement as that tiny yes came from my mouth.

It was done in such haste there hardly been even time to remember any details from the past few days with the weight of everything in front of me. Useless, time-wasting, specifics stuck around instead, like how long it took to fasten this doublet over my lacey shirt, and under a formal coat.

Now my day was filled with listening to the concerns of anyone who wrote or pilgrimaged to what was once the Hart's castle. By lunch, I realized how contradictory many requests were. The poor man who wanted a cow thought it was fair for it be given from the barren land of another. The cow's owner wanted better land, and the cow was meant to aid in a quest to get there. And so on, and so on.

When I finally got time to try to figure things out for others, the merry men had their own set of wishes. For one, the end of the hired House of Cards. Humphry spent his afternoon scribbling a draft of their abolishment.

"This will be our show of faith," Robin said, as the ink of the paper was still drying. "That corruption must be torn down. Only then something new can be put in place to better protect people."

He was such a beautiful idealist. I wondered if his formal attire would be easier to rip off than mine had been to put on. "I'm not sure folks will believe the gesture of being 'among the people' dressed like this."

Humphrey exhaled sharply. "One must look the part, so people know who the authority in the room is."

I glanced to Robin, hoping he'd explain how he never had to wear such things to be a good leader. But his focus was on my hands.

My eyes dropped to the flowering pattern of the lace that only slipped an appearance out before stopping at my fingers. "You're into this?"

Robin flushed. "It is working on me."

Before I could take him off somewhere and ask him to prove it, a quill pen was shoved into sight. Humphrey's finger tapped where I was meant to sign.

I took the paper and shot him a look as he backed off a step. Humphrey cared about the law in a curious way, making it both his duty and plaything.

After reading the document, I did feel pride, and hoped more would follow to right other awfulness. For all my magic, there was a different type of power in being able to write the rules.

"We should have a ball!" Charming declared.

Thankfully, he had been helping me figure out this ruling thing. And all the norms that came with it, but...

"A ball?"

"It is customary to throw one when there's news to spread through a kingdom. It's quite a good way to get people to enjoy your rule. Maybe even understand that no Card can dictate their hand in life anymore."

I picked up a stack of letters. Wondering how many were even addressed to me. They could be for a woman who had been killed by someone who then was eaten for supper.

"Oh, oh!" Madison called, as if anyone thinking about death for too long gave him an idea. "Might I be of help and take care of the ball for you?"

I glanced at Robin, who shrugged. "There is a lot to do. And I'm not convinced of a celebration. But if it's the norm, then your help will make it so I can go over other things."

Robin vowed to help me sort the pile of requests. More of which were stacked on private back-room tables and cloth sacks.

"Just don't make this ball—" I searched for a word and came up with nothing that didn't sound personal. "Dead."

"It will be perfectly lively." Madison smiled and threw an arm around Charming as if they were in cahoots. The Prince politely removed his arm.

"I'll spread the word to the villages," Charming said.

It had been nearly a week. If not more, given the lack of sleep I was getting. In the Queen's study I had laid out everyone's request out trying to place them together like pieces all from the same puzzle.

"Sir?" Little John stuck his head into the room. "You asked for a reminder when the sun set."

"Right, thank you." After looking away for a second the pattern I was trying to connect felt weaker. With a sigh, I gave up and decided to go to the ball.

I walked out to an inner garden, expecting to find guests dressed in their finest. Proper as you'd ever seen them behaving, and dancing in tight careful circles.

Instead, the Hatter had failed to mention that this was a clothing optional affair. Five people or so, judging by the number of limbs that were tangled together on the grass.

Eager mouths found each other, and other things. No two seemed to be focusing on one person in particular in a rather quite free form exchange.

"Your Highness!"

I jumped. Embarrassment swept over me as I looked for the sound of the voice. Who could that be and how long did they catch me standing there?

The next chamber was a long hall with paintings and other trappings of wealth meant to show off how well the kingdom was doing. Even more people graced this area drinking, laughing, and stealing the art off the walls. This lot was better at keeping their clothes on.

"Finally," Madison said, breaking from the group he'd been standing with.

"What's going on here? Has everyone gone mad?"

"Precisely," the Hatter said leaning in. With a spinning grace, he picked a drink up from the nearest table and offered the porcelain cup and saucer. "Tea, my king?"

For decades, when I used to pine over Robin, I'd try to decode his expression. Figure out if a glance my way meant he liked me. And if he did like me, was it enough to ever let me put my mouth on his? The Hatter was nothing like that. Desires seemingly as clear as the people fucking on the side lawn. "Just the drink."

"Why of course," Madison continued, playing innocent. "Two kings are a very good hand; I'd never split the pair."

"Wouldn't three of a kind be better?"

He bopped me on the nose, and I nearly dropped the tea in my surprise. "Naughty, naughty," Madison grinned, and started to walk away. "It all really depends on what game you're playing. In blackjack you would bust."

I just shook my head and watched him vanish into the party. Remembering the drink and took a sip. Fruity, like lemon that didn't make your cheeks tighten.

Within a moment the world divided into three overlaid versions of itself. Whatever predominate color something was had an after image of a different shade on each side. It was a dizzying effect and I put the cup down so I wouldn't stumble.

As soon as the saucer left my hand, my vision cleared. Curious. I picked it back up, studying the floral design for anything overtly magical. After not seeing anything, I brought the cup up to my lips and tried again.

This new colorful world was less disorienting the second time. I still felt dizzy, but in a fun tipsy way after I got a feel for it. I decided to spend the rest of the night attempting to find the most interesting object in the castle.

It didn't take me long to conclude that smashing all the Queen's breakable things made the best effect. Take the white vases lining the audience chambers. Not remarkably interesting on their own. Throw them on the ground and they suddenly erupted with a cascading rainbow. Soon other random townsfolk decided they too wanted to take their anger out instead of stealing stuff joined in and it was a jolly good riot.

I found Robin in a room off from the throne and swung my arm around his shoulder, deciding if anyone had a problem, they could leave my house.

"How do you think he does it?" I asked.

"Who does what?" Robin was holding a book sideways, so maybe I should have asked someone else.

"Make the tea stop."

"What?" He laughed. "Do you want it to stop?"

"Not really."

He dropped the book, bored with it now. "Then I wouldn't worry about it."

I watched as a couple stumbled in. The woman giggling as they rapidly undressed themselves seemingly without a care in the world that there were at least half a dozen people in here with them. "We should move."

Robin glanced up, stunned still for a moment before he got up in agreement. We hung out in the throne room which was filled with mostly drinking and dancing. Without any decorum people went everywhere that wasn't guarded and with us being the authority very few places still were.

There was no reason this palace needed to be a private museum. To have pantries filled to the brim with salted food and closets upon closets full of silk was a waste for the two of us. This castle was as much, if not more, theirs. Let them have their fill.

Chapter Nineteen

Being a good leader wasn't just parties. But I did have just an ounce, and not a drop more, of understanding why so many made it an endless celebration of themselves.

What most had considered a nothing town that sat outside the Queen's castle was actually full of vibrant artists. Weavers, painters, and builders. Now that all the water in the area wasn't being diverted to keep the Queen of Hearts' decadent landscape alive, they had endless ideas on how to make their town itself have more green spaces.

The work was hopeful, but dreadfully slow. And often beyond my depth as someone whose botany knowledge only went as far was living within the tree line. We spent all day deciding what material was best to build with.

The candles were all burnt out by time I headed towards bed. Guiding myself through the halls by memory and moonlight.

Robin came in shortly after. He pulled his waistcoat off the second he entered our private chambers, letting it drop to the ground. I sighed thinking it would end up being another thing I had to clean up.

I stole a glance towards him from the journal I was recording the events of the day in. "Not tonight, Robin. I'm too tired to pull on magic." I cringed at my wording. That sounded like a poor euphemism. Giving up on any ceremony, I dropped the notebook onto a pile of books on the table. Most of them stayed there. One slid off the others and onto the floor.

"Then don't," Robin said. He came around and blocked me from picking it up. "No more work tonight. Let me serve our new king."

I smiled while rolling my eyes. If I hadn't been putting in the hours, I would have completely scoffed at the title. "I'd rather you just be Robin."

"Always with you." He tilted his chin towards the bed. It was a simple gesture that made me laugh.

I sat on the edge watching him carefully. His fingers brushed over the black lace and slid under my sleeve as if ever so softly testing how much of the delicate fabric existed. "I'm not fragile."

"Don't I know it, love."

Every inch of me felt excited at that word. But no magic came, just Robin stepping closer to undo the metal fasteners running along my shirt.

His own clothes were definitely less restrictive. I could easily find the scar above his hip bone. And savored the memory of knowing exactly when he got it, since I had been there as a kid. We'd been together for years before this moment where I could finally have and hold him.

If people ever wrote about our reign, they'd never know that story like I did. The weight of the memory was almost as comforting as the pressure from his legs straddling me.

I tried to kiss him, catching his lips just barely, held back by a hand on my bare chest. He pushed until I was pinned down to the bed. "You don't have to do a thing."

Being manhandled while knowing I could safely hurt with someone made my hips tense up into him. Cock hard and ready for his every promise, every pleasure his touch offered.

He undid the laces on his pants, and actually found mine easier to expose everything, but took neither pair off further. "Hold on."

Robin moved away for a moment. Messing with something by the sound of it. I didn't care to look to be sure. Robin came back moving my legs so he could step between. He tugged at my pants, and I arched my back to help him pull them down further. "Good boy," he teased.

"Don't ca-," I started, thought completely lost as he slipped two slick fingers in. My body shivered before my mouth worked again. "Don't stop," I corrected myself.

Forget foreplay when I was already eager for more. Robin hadn't been slow, hadn't taken it one finger at a time. Just took what he wanted with a smooth glide. Anyone else attempting that would have been thoughtlessly rough without consideration of what I could handle. Somehow Robin made sure my body would be able to take him.

"Along with the royal's hoarded wine, they stockpiled bottles of lube," Robin explained. He could have told me he had magical sex hands and I would have agreed if it meant he kept going. No awkward fumbling, no using just spit. The rich had this part of life figured out.

With the next thrust, his fingers slid further. My hands dug into the plush blankets around me. They gave away to me like my body was begging to give under Robin.

"I got you, Mal."

My eyes were crossing and all I could do is nod my belief of that fact.

Robin pulled back taking everything with him, making me suddenly drunk to get it back. "Ah, ah." He scolded as I started to sit up. Refusing to finish pulling his own pants off until I settled back down.

I licked my lips. Picturing what Robin's dick would feel like based on the fingers before. My fantasies hadn't gone far enough. Misjudged the pure size he had. How easy the lube made his every move nothing but pleasure. Him inside me was filling a hunger I hadn't been ever able to feed before. "Fuck me, Robin."

His hands dug into my hips and a small sound of approval escaped his throat. The sound joined in with my ragged breathing as he thrusted, and the bed creaked with the force.

I sat up just enough to take on the sight of my cock pressed up along his hip. Riding out each building pump along with the rest of my pleasure-shocked body. I threw my head back, teetering happily between this and outright coming. "I'm going to..."

There was the smile in the sound of his breath. "Are you asking for permission?"

"Yes. Please. Oh, please," I begged.

"Alright, let's see it."

I greedily took it all, until my legs tightened around his waist. I came between our warm bodies, and when I thought I couldn't take any more pleasure he tensed, leaned in, and moaned his own finish along with me.

"That..." I needed to catch my breath between words. "I've decided. Being king isn't all bad."

Robin collapsed next to me. "I'm having the best time

of my life."

Chapter Twenty

Anything is sustainable for a while, but my first thought today was that I don't get paid enough for this. Technically, I didn't even get paid. Simply got to claim stuff and order people to do things.

Holding a court for any complaints was good for a ruler to do, but people started to bring their personal problems, their own moral judgments, and impossible deadlines.

"Alright, there's five more for today," Robin said, schedule in hand.

Polaris lay at my feet looking as if he wanted a walk. I wondered if I could just sign away my crown. Plop it on Robin's head who was clearly enjoying this more than me. I stared out the window wishing to smell the freshly cut grass.

"The issues ranged from crops not growing to if we could turn the unused seasonal castles into homeless shelters."

"Wait, who petitioned that last one?"

Robin grinned. "I was thinking about it when that man kept going needlessly on about windmills. What do you think?"

"Brilliant."

He flushed, and the whole world felt slightly more tolerable to me. "I'll make sure people look into it. For now, let's finish up here."

"Confess what you've turned into!" A voice shouted as they stormed inside. The merry men helping out seemed confused if they should haul off the young girl. She was wearing a blue and white dress, outfit topped off with bright blonde hair.

Instead of yelling more, she respectfully came to a halt where the others had. "Wolf King," she said softer now. "My name is Alice. I've written to you and nothing. Now my demands are far more."

Robin stepped forward, in front of me and Polaris on the dais. He shifted the quiver strapped to his side that had been untouched for weeks. "And what might those be?"

Alice stared back in silent contest for a moment before taking a step to the side. Her shadow stayed fixed on the ground until a familiar figure grew from it.

I rose to my feet to face Madison, ignoring the girl all together. "And who might you be today?"

"Consider me a stone," he taunted, as Polaris snarled a warning.

Every nerve told me not to trust him. "Why are you here? Does this teenager wish to rule?"

"Don't be silly, Mal. People don't just become Queen." His smile was wide, amused to the last.

Magic pooled in my palm, dripping off my fingertips.

The Hatter gently placed his hands on Alice's back, scooting her forward and in front of him again. "She just wants to go home."

"This is a strange land you have," Alice said, clueless more than a threat. "I'm not sure I'm meant to be here."

I sighed. Flexing my hand and willing the rage to seep back from the forefront of my thoughts. "That's why you brought her to me? Thinking I'd empathize?"

Madison leaned in over her shoulder. Their height difference more noticeable in the effort. The girl must have been still a teenager. "Don't you?"

Robin scuffed. "This is nonsense."

"You're up to something, Hatter. No one changes sides this often without their own agenda. And I'm going to figure out what that is."

Madison pulled his hands back to his chest to feign injury. "I merely wished to see if the Big Bad Wolf King was following the same patterns as before."

"Just stop." Robin readied his bow, holding it low in final warning. "Get out of our house."

Alice glanced up to the Hatter. "We should learn not to make such personal remarks," she said, more soberly than her intentional yelling before. "It's rude."

"Perhaps, dear child," he said, eyes breaking from mine.

My heart pounded anticipating an attack. "This isn't over."

"We'll see." He took off his hat and just as he dropped it on her head, they both vanished in a puff a magic.

Chapter Twenty-One

One does not fully live until they go castle shopping with their boyfriend. We had been held up in a building we literally won. But we now traveled with Jonathan, and Sophie, touring the other three seasonal mansions. Guided by staff of each that wished us to stay, since they had grown used to getting more food when the Queen of Hearts visited.

In the spring castle, confusion broke out when they heard Robin and I talk about which would be best to live in, and which would better fit our own grand ideas. Some of the staff seemed pleased at the idea of homeless people living among them. Taking care of someone who needed a hand, instead of just following demands on threat of death.

But not everyone was loving our ideas. Robin politely suggested everyone treat them like they would us or could kindly not show up the following day. For his quick wit, I gave him a fleeting kiss on his cheek as one prissy court hand scoffed at our lack of modesty.

The plight of those who thought they were better than the hungriest peasant simply because they served royalty meant nothing to me. These positions were rarely earned, instead given to a family line. Passed down and jealously guarded by people that had come before.

I wasn't sure what was going to happen when I explained to a chef the new menu we wanted. Soups, and anything that could be made in large batches and sent out.

"No tarts? Or chocolate sculptures?" the man asked, apron dirty with a coat of flower.

"I'm sure you do a fine job making them," Robin soothed. "But that isn't needed anymore."

When the chef's eyes watered, Robin grew confused, looking to me for guidance as the man wiped away the unshed tears.

"Thank you, Kings." He bowed deeply, the pause giving us a moment. "Every day I see my neighbors go hungry while I'm forced to throw away desserts that aren't a perfect work of art."

Once Robin and I were walking alone, I pushed him up against a wall to honor that bit of joy he created for someone. Tracing my tongue along his mouth as if to memorize the wonderous things they could speak into existence.

We were late to leave for the winter estate solely because Robin decided he had more than kissing in mind as he placed a hand on the small of my back and pulled me flush against him. To think we had gone our whole lives without the indulgence of each other. Always willing to risk our lives for each other, but never our friendship.

This last castle was nothing like the others. Those at least pretended to be accessible to people. In no way was this wintery land designed to hold balls or guests deemed as important.

Our horses stopped a way off with only the large building on the horizon, sitting on a raised mountainous outcrop in the middle of a labyrinth laid out around it. Hedges were set in unnaturally sharp angles stretching the otherwise short distance as long as physically possible.

"Do you know the path?" I asked our guide.

He shook his head. "This is as far as I ever get. When I used to deliver the Queen of Hearts someone would come out to greet us. They were able to control the maze."

The only other landmarks I could see from the ground were jagged rocks to the far side, and an extraordinary large tree within the maze. The branches alone looked as large as me. "What do you think, Robin? If there is one on each side, they might serve as a compass."

He said nothing as he dismounted his horse. Positioning himself towards the sun and gauging what direction the tree appeared. "Yeah, this must be East."

"Do we go in ourselves?" Jonathan asked.

"We wrote that we were coming but heard no word," our guide said meekly.

I got off my horse doubting a hedge maze would be much more than an annoyance. "We'll figure it out from here."

The four of us ventured in. First taking a path that forked off the left, and quickly found our first dead end. After backtracking, and trying a new way, we started to make clear progress.

The path opened wider to form a room of sorts. In the middle, serving as a marker that I assumed meant Northeast was a marble statue of the Queen of Hearts.

"I had it all wrong," Jonathan mumbled, staring up at it. "Thought the title was virtuous. That she needed protection, but she was just awful. Withholding from everyone for herself. All a contest to acquire as many pretty things as possible."

"None of this is a game," Robin said.

"To them it is. I bet when she got bored of listening, she came here, making it hard for anyone to say another word. Freeze them out."

My eyes lifted to the sun which was threatening to set below our sight line. "We need to keep moving."

We walked faster. Several dead ends later I feared the area was out of season and not kept in a fashion that actually had a solution.

"Bunny!" Sophie pointed to a white rabbit. It jumped as it was spotted by all of us and ran off. Quickly followed by Sophie, and everyone else either trying to get her to stop like Jonathan. Or thinking it might be the way out, like me.

There was something magical about this place. About her. I decided to simply trust it.

Sophie lost sight of the rabbit as he dropped into a hole already dug under a hedge. But faith had rewarded us with a winding hedge-less path up to the castle.

"What did I tell you before about running off?" Jonathan scolded.

"Not without taking you with me." She pouted, trying to be cute enough not to be in too much trouble. Given that she did find the way out, it would probably work.

I didn't have the heart to tell Jonathan right then that

Sophie was probably a mage too. Especially now that we were standing in front of a spire building that looked more holy than regal.

This one building sat alone. Secluded to the last it seemed. No stables. No maids quarter. Inside large arched doors sat an echoing room with tables along the sides. Somewhere there must be stairs leading up to rooms above, but I didn't see them from here.

Three people stood over a body lied out on a bench off to a side. Slightly obscured by a large pillar until we moved closer. A woman was crouched down, her hand on the injured child's arm trying to soothe him. Another man paced. Hand to his mouth, arms crossed. It looked like he wanted to offer help, but nothing came to mind. Light glowed under the hands of the last. The magic illuminated the dust in the air between him and the lying body.

The healer looked up and our way. One eye a swirling color, the other nothing, absolutely average. "If you are the new king, we wish to have no part of it."

Of that much I was certain, could feel it in my bones as confidently as the stranger spoke. "Is this a hospital?"

"Of sorts."

With that he went back to treating the child before him. I saw magic pulse against his chest in waves. With a gasp, the kid woke.

The worried glances at us were instead poured into focusing on the miracle that their son was moving. "Is he going to be okay, Warren?"

The healer nodded. "Just try to keep him away from the bell tower." Warren walked around the bench to stand protectively in front of the family. "This castle may be yours. But it's occupied."

"Claiming squatter's rights?" Jonathan asked.

Sophie lifted on her toes to get a better look. "What happened to him?"

Warren ignored the elder sibling. "He became too frightened, and his heart stopped. Now please leave. There is wild magic in these parts, and we don't need any more patients."

His tone sounded near threat so I spoke my words as softly as I could. "What do you need?"

He laughed, like the idea of being offered anything was unfathomable. "For the crown to give, instead of take."

"Supplies. Food. The deed to this place. It can be all yours."

Warren narrowed his eyes. "And your price?"

I brought up my hands gesturing to the hall. "This would make a fine school."

"You're nothing like the Queen, are you? What do you wish to enroll the youth among you?" Warren started to walk away, picking up stray items left on the benches.

"Her and any mage who needs help."

Warren's movements slowed to a halt. "You're not playing?"

"Malcolm and I," Robin said, "have been traveling to see the best ways to change things. Seems your new Wolf King wishes your aid in building fresh."

"Do I have to kneel and pledge my loyalty?"

I grinned. "Only if you *really* like me."

Warren laughed, the sound breaking the remaining tension. "Let me show you around."

Whatever my legacy would become it started here. Plans took several months, and complete dedication to laying the groundwork in place. I stayed in the winter castle and sent for Polaris. While Robin and his merry men divided their time on repurposing castles to become still quite lavish community centers.

My focus was on the university. Working to study the theory of how the Hatter, Warren, I, and others were able to be mages in the first place. While the goal was a safe environment, it felt better having a healer around.

The nine lands had plenty of fancy buildings, what it completely lacked was somewhere for healing, rest, and training for people to test their capabilities. The Beast had given me a familiar and made it clear to me that he was an animal shaped crutch. Others may need help in similar or different ways.

The Queen had been using this place to have a quiet retreat to retire, now anyone burnt out had somewhere to put their head down.

The days were manageable because I had a mission. But every night, I longed for Robin to be at my side. For somewhere we could be together again. My quarters were made from a royal sized walk-in closet. Big enough for a cot, desk, and walking space to reach them both and a rectangle window that let a slice of light in.

Sophie had a similar one. It was too impersonal for her liking and she spent most of her time in the numerous connected studies.

Instead of fancy parties, the bell tower would ring at sunrise. Whispering the correct path through the labyrinth. Every day before breakfast I'd argue with Warren if it was accessible enough to the people we were trying to help.

It had become so routine that the morning it didn't happen there was no sense of victory, and I went to go find where he'd gone.

I found him by a side garden talking with someone.

"Can you teach me what this seed can do?" a young boy asked.

Warren leaned forward, holding his hands out to take the odd-looking sprout. "Where did you find this?"

"A man with a top hat gave it to me. He said it was a baby beanstalk."

"Jack, beanstalks don't have seeds."

I forced myself to appear nonchalant, stuffing hands that wanted to curl up into fists into my pockets. "Did you say a top hat?"

Jack nodded. "He said I could plant it wherever I wanted, and it would grant me a wish."

Warren eyed me over. "Do you know someone like that?"

"Yes, a necromancer."

"Oh." He stood up straighter. Holding the seed up to the sunlight trying to understand it better. "That's a strange form of healing."

We took the seed to the bell tower, promising a favor instead. Thankfully, Jack hadn't had anything in mind to wish for, so he agreed.

The seedling sat in a ray of sunlight. It's large brown bulb still had dirt on it. The tip of the seed had already sprouted a dark green head.

"Warren, do you know anything about these?"

164

"Hmm?" He glanced up, question clicking afterward. "Beanstalks only grow in this area. You can see an outcrop from here actually."

I looked out from the tower. Over a small river dotted with a few trees to the far distance past a small village to where thick stalks grew into the cloud line. The Mad Hatter had to be there.

Warren brushed the dirt off with his hand. "Kind of looks like a potato wanting to root."

That was almost it, but too random. And not quite the thought lingering in my head. In one of the books we pulled down from storage, there had been an oval shape with wisps curling up encased in a triangle. At the time, I thought it had been fire. But given another sprout or two lifting up and this fledgling beanstalk could grow to look exactly the same. Could they be related somehow?

"The hedges are manmade," Warren rambled. "They used to change based on the directions of a mage here. Unlike them, beanstalks carry their own magic. The only reason they aren't farmed is an adult stalk is too thick to cut down. And they don't drop seeds, so there's never any new growth to harvest."

"Something's changed."

As Warren nodded, I pulled up my sleeves. The magic that had marked me might hold a clue given the right frame to put it into context. Finding nothing that stood out on my arms, I peeled off the jacket, then started unbuttoning the shirt.

"Yeah, I'm not sure I trust this thin—" Warren glanced up, shock lasting enough for the gears in his head to turn forward a new thought. "Whoa, what are you doing?"

Ignoring him, I pulled up my undershirt. "Here, look." On my ribs were three separate symbols. Smaller in size than the rest, unless you put them together like a constellation. "Can you get some ink?"

Warren quickly got on the same page as me. He grabbed a brush and drew a line across my skin. Starting at a hollow circle shape then towards three wavy lines that appeared to be smoke. Then added a line connecting them both to a lower symbol that looked like an x that crossed near the top.

I stared down at the inverted triangle feeling as if I suddenly found forbidden knowledge. Like the old book had lost its labels and I had them etched onto me.

"What does it mean?"

"Where there is smoke…" I brought my hand up to my eye line. Letting the magic free and drag upwards in the air. With a hot breath I blew and magic crackled and sparked into a flame. Red, orange, and warm. Unlike anything I'd created myself before. "There is fire."

"Holy shit," Warren said, as he stood up equally fascinated by what was in my hand. "I didn't know you could create things like that."

"Neither did I."

Warren glanced back towards the seed. Sucking through his teeth before he let out a frustrated groan. "Get rid of the seedling. We can't trust what it could bring here, or what it could do."

"You sure?"

"Everything burns, Mal."

Whatever Madison was up to I could stop him. The

166

rumors of strange happenings continued. But, I found myself too busy teaching strangers and too eager for Robin's upcoming visit to track down more problems for the time being.

When Robin made it back, we pushed two cots together. The downgrade in living conditions felt most noticeable with the middle two edges digging into my back. I simply didn't want to object as Robin was lying with his head on my chest.

"That chef has been traveling around with us. He's eager to teach others how to make simple things in town tomorrow. We brought along a cart worth of supplies."

My happy hum to show I was listening ended short. "Wait, you're leaving so soon?"

"You didn't hear we were heading out?"

"No." I shifted uncomfortably, trying not to move too much and ruin what little peace I had.

"Oh, sorry. Guess we don't have much time to talk lately."

In the morning, we had rolled to our own side of each cot. My first thought was enough. Enough of this, and every other thing nagging at me. I got up and decided to focus on my own wishes and left without waking him up.

Chapter Twenty-Two

Fire followed me out. Eating away the needless maze surrounding the castle that only made people work for a moment of relief. It caught the compass tree, turning leaves to soot, as the damage brought down the trunk. No more half measures, or literal barriers to entry to a place of education and healing.

Now to solve the threat on its borders. Polaris and I trekked through the swampland that surrounded the only known grove of beanstalks. The area smelled of wet soil. Here any flame burned out, the land too moist to allow itself to become kindling.

The beanstalks full height was hidden from us by ceaseless cloud cover. That visual trick is what made them appear even more ageless. Any new growth was hidden out of sight.

The area would often shake in paired sets of earthquakes from the stalks down. Polaris' four legs being lower to the ground was having an easier time not tripping as we hunted.

A rope hung from one of the beanstalks. I moved close enough to give it a tug, and it seemed secure enough to climb up. Someone was around for sure.

"You are making a mistake." A voice called along with another quake. Once the earth settled, I realized it hadn't been someone from above.

"Don't start this tale over, Wolf," Madison warned. Today, the Hatter was missing his signature accessory. Shirt rolled up past the elbow and forearms covered with damp soil, holding a bucket with something small and green peeking out.

"You worked with Red against the crown," I said, stalking closer. "Possessed dead things. Killed people. Wasted my time. Now you take seeds from the only known place of natural magic."

"That was war."

"And what's this?" I stretched my arms out to everything growing around us. Not a single new bloom in sight just thick tall stalks.

His mouth twitched, saying nothing.

"You played with people's lives! Their bodies, their... everything treated like your toys. Nothing new has sprouted here in centuries. For the last time, tell me what you are doing."

He let go of the pail. Looking me over from head to toe before his eyes dropped to my familiar. "You mean to stop me?"

"Yes."

"There's still so much you don't know about magic. To you it's this infinite wonderful thing full of imagination." He started, closing the distance between us. "To me, it's death. Decay. Timelessness. And time. Ho-ho, now that's an even

169

more difficult beast."

He was in my face and it hardly mattered since distance didn't mean much with people like us. "But when I have tea, it's all laid out in rippling threads through time. Would you like your future?"

"I make my destiny."

"You sure do." There was pity in his tone. "I can show you how the story goes if you continue throwing yourself into things for everyone but yourself." His words were anything but friendly and a hand seized the back of my head.

I was unable to pull away as a shimmer from his other hand whispered images into my mind. Magic which once gave me everything I desired, now providing nothing but a skull splitting headache. Trapped between my skin and bones, searching for a way out. A crack where pain couldn't reach.

Madison's voice narrated, guiding every thought and sight. Making me mad for the making. "The other Hart's resent your rule. A break in the long chain of their lineage. It starts with Sophie. Poisoned by an apple as she plays with Snow White's own child. Done to convince you to sign away some freedoms least there be more attacks on those you care about. She lies in state for years.

"Cirrus so filled with guilt, dedicates his life to finding a cure. But nothing is found. Jonathan moves on first. Taking to the seas with nothing but piracy left in his heart.

"On the verge on giving up, Cirrus weeps over Sophie's coffin. He pushes the glass lid away. Knowing he's failed. With a kiss goodbye, her eyes finally open. Love always wins. Somewhere, at least."

An animal trapped in a snare fighting to wake up. That's all that was left of me. And barely that.

"And your Robin," he says.

Robin sat getting ready in front of a vanity left from the last owner. It's grand and golden shape transposed in between swamp. "When did you pick up such an intricate looking comb?"

I looked down as if nothing strange was occurring, to jot down notes about something else. "What's that?"

Robin winced. And as I looked back up, he's holding his hand strangely. Drops of blood beaded up. "Did you cut yourself?"

He grew pale before the whites of his eyes rolled up. Then just as suddenly all the images were blown apart by the breeze.

I jerked against Madison's control. Nightmare or not, I could save him. I...

"Look at you now. So full of love," he continued, maddeningly true to his name.

"Why are you doing this," I growled, as tears escaped from my eyes. "What do you want?"

"For now, let's just say I want a happy ending. Prevent all that awfulness from happening in the first place. It can be my gift to you."

Anger rooted my voice, making sure the words didn't waver. "I don't trust you."

"You don't have to."

In a flash his hand phased through my chest. I stared at the missing limb that had taken a grip on my heart. With a tug, he pulled his hand back out, taking the beating thing with him. "You've already given this away."

Standing on my own was an impossibility at this point. And I slumped forward into Madison, grabbing onto him to steady myself. Over his shoulder I saw Robin again, and Polaris' barking.

171

Magic was the only thing keeping me alive. If I could even call having each sense blink out after hitting a painful limit living.

"Now don't be a martyr." The voice was cruel, even as it tries to help. "It will make this all the more difficult."

The smell of pine and fresh air. "Mal, I'm not letting you go." I could feel the wind on my face. The dream image must have returned.

"Robin?" My lips hurt, like they'd crack if I'd tried to speak again. "Didn't you leave?"

"I followed you out of the castle. Stay with me."

My chest sharply ached and I reached a hand towards it.

"Careful with that," said the first voice. "That necklace now holds your mortality."

Spite more than anything else brought consciousness back. Around my neck sat a coin on a leather rope.

Robin pulled one of my arms over his shoulder and angled us towards the Hatter. "You couldn't have left it inside him?"

He shrugged a shoulder half-heartedly. "I made your love virtually immortal now. A thank you would be nice."

My life being melted down into a piece of metal seemed worth another look. On the face was a crowned skull. On the reverse side, letters were written in a downward spiral. "A Dead King's Peace. Posthumous Service Medal."

"You think that's funny?" Robin scolded further.

"Yes." Madison looked unbothered that we didn't see the humor. "What can I say? I'm a romantic through and through. Wanted the ending where you two got to stay together forever. The only way that was possible was for you to die and create a new power vacuum. Oh, things in

Wonderland are about to get truly mad."

"Us staying together?" Robin repeated, turning his head to me. The weight of realizing that he hadn't ever seen a different fate for us was painful in a way that made me know we were both alive.

I tucked the necklace under my shirt just in case that mad man decided to take it back. "How long was I dead for?"

"A bit." He hardly gave me any attention before making a tsking sound. "Your little Big Bad here, was about to throw himself at a losing battle. Again. I had to make sure he learned to fight for the life he actually wanted."

"By killing me?"

"Some cycles must be broken."

"Thank you." Robin interrupted, seemingly half a conversation behind. He pressed his forehead to my temple. "We didn't need to save the lands forever. Just be a part of fixing it."

"Anyway, the kingdom will be in shambles." Madison lifted his voice, bouncing on the balls of his heels as if trying to tempt us to ask more. "Your little new magical college won't know what to do with itself. Oh, but what they could learn. Pure anarchy. Someone really should do something about all of that."

I nuzzled closer to Robin. "They will have to find someone else."

"That's right." Robin smiled, even laughed as Polaris barked an echoed agreement.

"I love you." The three words I had neglected to say. Something I'd never forget to show again. The greatest truth I've ever known and then kissed the boy I had always adored. Today, tomorrow, and happily ever after.

READ MORE BIG BAD MAGIC IN
THE 9TH PAWN

**In that direction lives a Hatter:
and in that direction lives a Frog Prince.
Visit either you like: they're both madly in love.**

Madison is a simple hatter fulfilling the whims of the fussy aristocracy. Or at least he's pretty sure he was in one lifetime. Now more of an Alice guiding, antique owning, crown killer with a penchant for necromancy.

After meeting a curious prince named Henri, Madison is ready to kiss as many frogs as it takes to win his heart. He's never encountered anyone as worthy of love. But to prove his sincerity, Madison must help stabilize the Wonderland he helped tear apart.

Their romance is forbidden by the Hatter's agelessness and the Prince's duty to produce an heir. Madison can see Henri wants to choose differently — but wanting and choosing are different things when a crown is involved.

Continue the love with THE 9TH PAWN!

ABOUT THE AUTHOR

Rose Sinclair writes stories filled with big magic, underworld romance, and queer characters who refuse to play by the rules. A community leader and activist at heart, they've spent over a decade shaking things up for LGBTQIA+ representation and building decentralized support networks. When they aren't busy masterminding their next fictional universe or hunting down rare trading cards, they can be found hanging out online. Connect with Rose on Instagram @RoseOverChaos.